FISH SHOOT

The President was standing tall on the platform, making his speech. Canyon wasn't paying attention to it. Every fiber of him was tuned into the crowd at the railway station.

Then he heard it. The crack of a high-powered rifle. His head turned in the direction of the sound. He heard screams, and spotted a puff of blue smoke. It rose from the roof of a small store across the street, not more than sixty yards from the President.

Shooting fish in a barrel range! Canyon thought as he whipped out his own gun and started sprinting after the shooter.

The death trip had begun—on a track heading straight for disaster.

CANYON O'GRADY

12

RAILROAD RENEGADES

by

Jon Sharpe

A SIGNET BOOK

SIGNET
Published by the Penguin Group
Penguin Books USA Inc., 375 Hudson Street,
New York, New York 10014, U.S.A.
Penguin Books Ltd, 27 Wrights Lane,
London W8 5TZ, England
Penguin Books Australia Ltd, Ringwood,
Victoria, Australia
Penguin Books Canada Ltd, 2801 John Street,
Markham, Ontario, Canada L3R 1B4
Penguin Books (N.Z.) Ltd, 182-190 Wairau Road,
Auckland 10, New Zealand

Penguin Books Ltd, Registered Offices:
Harmondsworth, Middlesex, England

First published by Signet, an imprint of New American Library,
a division of Penguin Books USA Inc.

First Printing, March, 1991
10 9 8 7 6 5 4 3 2 1

The first chapter of this book previously appeared in *Soldier's Song*,
the eleventh volume in this series.

 REGISTERED TRADEMARK—MARCA REGISTRADA

Printed in the United States of America

PUBLISHER'S NOTE
This is a work of fiction. Names, characters, places, and incidents either are
the product of the author's imagination or are used fictitiously, and any resem-
blance to actual persons, living or dead, events, or locales is entirely coincidental.

Canyon O'Grady

His was a heritage of blackguards and poets, fighters and lovers, men who could draw a pistol and bed a lass with the same ease.

Freedom was a cry seared into Canyon O'Grady, justice a banner of his heart.

With the great wave of those who fled to America, the new land of hope and heartbreak, solace and savagery, he came to ride the untamed wildness of the Old West.

With a smile or a six-gun, Canyon O'Grady became a name feared by some and welcomed by others, but remembered by all . . .

February 3, 1861 . . . seven hundred miles from Washington, D.C., to Chicago, and every mile could be a death trap for President James Buchanan unless Canyon O'Grady could put out the fuse set by the deadly Blue Goose Lodge . . .

1

Major General Rufus Wheeler shook his head at the President of the United States as they both stood in the gently swaying private railroad car that rolled along the sometimes uneven tracks from Washington, D.C., toward Pennsylvania.

"Mr. President, I'm recommending that we bypass this small Pennsylvania town of Bixby and continue on to Lawton for our next stop. You've read the telegram from the sheriff at Bixby. He says he can't guarantee your safety there. He has only three deputies, and one of them is out sick. He expects three hundred people at the station."

President James Buchanan smiled at the three people who faced him. "I know you folks mean well, and you're doing the job I gave you. But we're just getting started on this trip. We haven't been on the rails for three hours yet. If we fail to stop at every town where there are a couple of folks who don't like me, we won't be stopping at any of the towns between here and Chicago."

"Sir," Canyon O'Grady said from where he leaned against the side of the private car outfitted especially for the president by the railroad. When Buchanan looked at Canyon, he continued.

"Mr. President, the telegram said specifically that there were three or four known troublemakers in Bixby and they had sworn that they would, 'Make President Buchanan forever remember this day and the town of Bixby, Pennsylvania.' That is a clear threat, sir. We can't ignore it.''

"Of course not,'' the president said as he sat down behind a desk that had been bolted to the floor. The chair had rollers on it and he pushed back two feet. He glanced at the only woman in the car.

"Miss Franklin, what do you make of this? Is it a threat or just some good old boys with a few too many beers out to have a fine time?''

Wendy Franklin was a new special agent in service with General Wheeler, and she was frankly nervous and a bit overwhelmed to be working so closely with the president. She hesitated a moment before she spoke.

"Mr. President, I'm not sure. But there is a good chance that it's a bona fide threat. I don't see how we can dismiss it, or worse yet, ignore it. I would recommend that we do not stop at Bixby.''

"Well,'' the president said, wiping one hand across his forehead and pushing back the snow-white hair that tufted high on his head. James Buchanan was known in Washington as the Bachelor President, and while he had never married, he had a keen and appreciating eye for a pretty girl. He sighed. The weight of nearly four years of the presidency bore down heavily on James Buchanan's frail shoulders. It was the first week in February, 1861, and this would be his last trip as president. Inauguration of President-elect Abraham Lincoln was coming up March 4, only four weeks away.

Buchanan peaked his fingers in front of his face and looked at each of the people in turn. "I thank you all for your advice, but the decision is up to me. That's why I'm president. We'll stick to the approved schedule and stop at Bixby—unless you can show me some concrete proof that there will be an attempt on my life at that stop.'' The president paused and looked around.

The three shook their heads.

''Mr. President, we don't have anything that sure. Still—'' General Wheeler began.

The president held up his hand. ''Then let's stop and enjoy the small town of Bixby. Oh, it's cold out there. Don't forget to bundle up a bit.''

The advisers withdrew to the second car of the three-car train. It was made up of the president's private sleeper car, the shorter observation/passenger car with a wide veranda-like platform in back from which the president would make his talks, and the engine up front.

General Wheeler looked at Canyon and signed. ''What the hell can we do now?''

''We make sure nobody shoots the president,'' Canyon said.

The twenty crack army guards lounged in the car's seats, waiting for the next town. They were turned out in new uniforms, polished boots, and well-oiled rifles. Each also had a percussion pistol on a wide leather belt.

''I'll tell the lieutenant that we're stopping,'' Canyon said. ''Wendy and I will get off the front of the president's car the minute it hits the station, and work both sides of the platform. I'll have the lieutenant put his men around the rear of the car to keep the crowd back at least ten yards from the end of the observation car. We'll have the honor guard standing with their rifles at port arms. Wendy and I will work the crowd, mingle in it, and be watching for anyone who looks suspicious. As on the last stop, General, you'll be on the platform with the president.

''I'm sure the sheriff and his deputies will be in the crowd as well. Our big problem is if there is somebody out there who wants to hurt the president, we can't do anything until he makes the first move.''

"We should go on through Bixby," Wendy Franklin said. "I just have a feeling about this place." Wendy watched General Wheeler. She was nearly five feet, six inches. Taller than most of the other women she knew. She was slender, with long blond hair and soft brown eyes.

"Feelings won't help us much if somebody starts shooting," Canyon said with a little more bite than he had intended. "Be sure you have that six-gun of yours behind a fold in your skirt so you can get it up in a rush.''

"I know my job, O'Grady," Wendy said with a touch of sharpness.

General Wheeler scowled at them. The general was a rather short man alongside Canyon. He stood just five feet, eight inches, and had added a few pounds each decade until he was a well-rounded man.

"Look, you two. We may have fight enough from somebody out there in Bixby. We don't need to do any battling in the ranks. Now stop it.''

"Right," Canyon said, and they felt the train start to slow. "I'm forward on the first car," he said, and hurried into the president's car and to the front of it and the doorway where a porter stood ready to open the door and put down a stepping stool. He saw Wendy on the other side ready to get off as well.

Canyon carried two revolvers on this trip. He had the familiar Colt 1860 percussion model .44 in his holster tied low on his right leg. He could fire it five times by cocking the hammer with his thumb between rounds. Then it took him about two minutes to reload the five cylinders one at a time with the linen loads of premeasured powder and ball that had to be rammed into each cylinder from the front.

It took more seconds to put the percussion caps on the nipples at the breach end of the cylinder, again one for each cylinder.

For insurance he now carried a new Smith & Wesson #2 revolver in a belt holster under his jacket. This weapon was only ten inches long and weighed twenty-three ounces. It was a six-round revolver of .32 caliber but had the advantage of using rim-fire solid metallic cartridges that could be reloaded quickly. It didn't have the range of hitting power of the larger weapon, but in close, it was deadly.

Canyon waited for the porter to drop off the car and jumped past him just before the train stopped. There was a crowd on the platform already and it surged forward to the frantic cries of the three sheriff deputies he saw there waving their arms. A light sifting of snow covered everything and the people wore heavy clothing. The temperature was near freezing.

Canyon watched his breath fog in front of him as he pulled his overcoat tighter around him and walked toward the crowd.

The people were curious, men and women, many holding small children so they could say they had seen in person the President of the United States.

Canyon settled the weapon in its side leather and walked toward one of the deputies.

"Keep everybody back ten yards from the president's car," O'Grady ordered, and the deputy with the silver star nodded.

The special agent of the U.S. government stared at the town of Bixby, Pennsylvania. The usual stores and shops and the few houses he could see looked normal. They were neat, well-kept and painted. The streets had been cleared of snow, and piles of it showed on the sides and in front of houses.

A man on a horse rode toward the crowd. Canyon

tensed, then he saw the man was simply rushing to get to see the president. He slid off his horse, tied it to a rail, and walked forward with the rest of the crowd.

Canyon eased into the throng, working toward the last car, where President Buchanan would be shortly. The mayor of Bixby was climbing to the observation car now, waving and shouting to the crowd. A hush fell on the throng.

Canyon figured there might be two hundred there, total. Not so many to worry about.

The mayor began to talk and welcome the people.

"Luke, get the hell out of the way and let President Buchanan come out," somebody yelled.

The mayor waved and motioned to General Wheeler, who nodded, and the president stepped forward and behind a podium that shielded him from the shoulders down.

James Buchanan was a modest-sized man with stark white hair, clean shaven with deep-set eyes and white, thick brows, a prominent nose, and a thin-lipped mouth.

He smiled at the crowd. As usual, he wore a high white collar, white shirt, black suit and vest. He had been a diplomat before he became president, and he looked the role.

"Good morning to all of you fine people of Bixby," the president said. "I'm glad we stopped here so I could talk to you. Thank you for coming out on this cold February morning to see me."

Canyon heard three horses pounding down the hard-packed dirt street. He turned and saw them coming, half a block away. The three men were roughly dressed and one pulled a revolver and fired a shot in the air.

Secret Agent Canyon O'Grady worked through the crowd toward the trio, who kept pounding forward directly at the gathering. They could ride right up to the back of the crowd, Canyon saw with a start. That would put them only forty yards from the president, well in range for a talented man with a good percussion revolver.

Canyon ran then, pushing people aside, rushing toward where the three riders would come in back of the crowd. One of the horsemen lifted a rifle. Canyon had his own Colt six-gun out and fired a shot over the man's head. The rider turned in amazement at Canyon and the rifle discharged into the air. Then he lowered it and Canyon stopped running. He was thirty yards from the men as they rode forward slower now, still too fast.

Canyon fired and his shot hit exactly where he wanted it to, in the charging horse's head between the eyes. The big sorrel went down like it had been hit with a sledgehammer.

Another rifle fired and Canyon turned and looked at the observation train car. General Wheeler dived to his right, slamming his body between the riflemen and President Buchanan.

Canyon didn't have time to find out what happened on the observation car. He lifted his six-gun again and charged toward the three horsemen, one of whom was now scrambling away from his dead mount. Canyon bellowed a warning and charged at the horsemen.

2

Four days ago in Washington, D.C., Canyon had been surprised when General Wheeler had told him about the new assignment.

"Someday there will be a department or agency that deals with the security of our president, but right now we don't have a single man assigned to that job. Hell, as a general with a division even, I had an honor guard of up to thirty of the best troops in the division who were my personal bodyguards. I couldn't even spit without them being there protecting me.

"Of course, the Caesars had their praetorian guards in the olden days. A mean, rough, and vicious group they were. That's why we need somebody right now to watch the president. He's going on a week trip to Chicago to open some kind of exhibition or fair or some damn thing."

"So you want me along to play bodyguard? I can't take the place of thirty armed troops."

"True, that's why we're getting twenty soldiers and a lieutenant assigned to help guard the president, at least for this trip. They'll come from the best army unit in Washington, top men who are tall and strong and who have seen action against the Indians. All of these twenty troopers know what their job is, and will obey orders without question."

"Then what's there for me to do, General Wheeler?

Shouldn't I be out West somewhere riding down some bad guys?''

"No, Canyon. You're supposed to be where you're ordered to be, just like any soldier. Making you a colonel for a month on that last mission of yours to Texas should have helped condition you on that aspect of government service. You'll be the expert on this trip, helping us take care of any problems in advance and then stopping any threats as they come up.''

"Do you know of any one or some group out there who wants to hurt the president?''

"We've had several threats, but presidents always get them. We're just not sure how serious they are—or if these individuals would try to travel with us or near us. His closest advisers have told the president not to make the trip. But he's overruled them, and we're still going. He says he only has a month left as president and he wants to do this in Chicago.''

"So, we take all the precautions that we can,'' Canyon said.

"Right. I'm bringing in another special agent to help. This agent hasn't been with us for very long but will be an asset.'' General Wheeler went to the door to his office, opened it, and talked for a moment, then held the door wide.

A slender, pretty girl with long blond hair came into the room. She looked at Canyon, then back at General Wheeler. "Yes, sir?''

"Wendy Franklin, I'd like you to meet Canyon O'Grady. The three of us will be working together on the train during the president's week-long trip to Chicago.''

"General, you said an agent—'' Canyon began.

"Yes, Wendy is a special agent, just the same as you, but without your experience. Up to about six months ago she worked with Edwin M. Stanton over at the attorney general's office. She's had a year in criminal investigation and had nearly finished her reading for the law when she decided to change professions. For the past six months she's been training with us."

Wendy held out her hand.

Canyon shook it gently and let go. "I didn't know we had any female agents," Canyon said. "This is quite a surprise."

"You've been in the field a lot lately, O'Grady."

"I assure you I can handle the job, Mr. O'Grady," Wendy said, color rising in her face.

"Perhaps most of it, Miss Franklin. Have you ever killed a man?"

"No."

"I have. Several. That's part of the required work in this job classification. I assume that General Wheeler told you all about that part of the job?"

"Not exactly, but I have a revolver and I can hit what I aim at."

"A cardboard target or a tree is a different situation than aiming and firing at another human being. Have you ever even shot at a man?"

"O'Grady, that will be enough of that," General Wheeler said sternly. "For now, let's say that you get to do any killing required."

"No," Wendy said. "Let's settle it. I'll wager five dollars that I can outshoot O'Grady right now on a target."

"It's a bet," Canyon said quickly. "The president set up a little target range behind the White House. Let's go out there right now."

General Wheeler scowled. "All right. Maybe that will be the best thing. Get this petty argument settled and then let's try to do some planning just how we're going to handle security around the president for the next week. That's our job right now, not some stupid little argument about guns."

"Begging your pardon, General, but my six-gun is what's kept me alive and working for you these past few years." Canyon looked at Wendy. "Let's go and do some shooting. I'd hope that you have your weapon with you?"

Wendy picked up her reticule and nodded. "Ready when you are, O'Grady."

Ten minutes later it was over. They had set up targets of descending size from a whiskey bottle on one end to a walnut on the small end. They put up identical targets against two different logs so each would have the same item to fire at.

"How far back?" Canyon asked.

"Thirty feet," Wendy said. She took from her reticule a curious weapon that Canyon had not seen before. He lifted his brows.

"It's a Plant-made revolver, converted to rimfire .41 caliber and it packs a good punch," Wendy said matter-of-factly. "It uses solid cartridges so I don't have to mess with caps and muzzle loading. Any other questions?"

Canyon shook his head, lifted his Colt, and blasted the whiskey bottle on his target into a hundred pieces.

Wendy did the same with her first round.

They traded shot for shot on the targets, each hitting the smaller ones in progression. At last only the walnut lay intact on each of the target logs.

"This time, ladies first," Canyon said.

Wendy lifted the big gun that had no trigger guard. She held the Plant revolver with both hands now, aimed, then let the weapon down to rest her arms a moment. Then she lifted the revolver, aimed, and fired.

She missed the walnut, coming close enough to turn it lazily in a circle once, but it was unharmed.

Canyon lifted his heavier Colt and fired almost at once. The walnut shattered.

"Nice shooting, Franklin," he said, and held out his hand. "I believe that you owe me five dollars."

Wendy's eyes flared for a moment, then she reached in her reticule and took out a five-dollar gold piece and handed it to him. She turned around and marched back to the rear door of the White House and down the hallway to General Wheeler's office.

The general looked up as the two came in. He didn't have to ask who won the bet. "Now maybe we can get down to work and figure out the best way to protect the president. In case you've forgotten, that's our job during that week-long trip to Chicago."

Now, four days later, Canyon O'Grady fired once more, this time over the heads of the two horsemen who had been charging toward the railroad car where President Buchanan was speaking.

"Stand steady," Canyon bellowed. "You men on horseback. You take another step and you're looking at hot lead."

The two men held their horses close-reined.

"Good. Now get down on my side of those mounts and stand like a pair of rocks."

He saw the other man beside his dead horse.

"You, without a mount, over with the others." When the three suspects were in a group, Canyon had time to look back at the president on the observation platform of the rail car.

General Wheeler was lying on top of the president on the floor of the car. The general looked around, ordered the troopers to pull back closer to the observation platform and keep their rifles at the ready.

There were no more shots. Dozens of the people there to see the president had dropped to the ground when the first shot had been fired. Now they stood and began looking around.

Wendy came out of the crowd near Canyon and quickly tied one of the three horsemen's hands behind his back. When all three had been tied, they were ordered to lay flat on their stomachs on the ground.

"Keep them here," Canyon told Wendy, and ran for the train. He got there in time to help President Buchanan up.

The president looked at General Wheeler and chuckled. "Rufus, you certainly take this protection assignment seriously, don't you?"

"Yes, sir, Mr. President, I do."

Canyon watched Buchanan a moment. "Sir, from the looks of the three we caught, they are half-drunk, and the only shots they made were into the sky. It looks like they had no intention of harming you."

"Told you so," President Buchanan said as he stepped back to the podium. The people cheered. He held up his hands for quiet. "Ladies and gentlemen, I hope none of you was hurt in that little excitement. Turns out we just had three young men celebrating a little too much. Now, let me say what I started to say before the guns started going off."

The president launched into the platform talk that he would give much the same way over and over again all the way to Chicago.

Canyon dropped off the car and hurried back to where Wendy stood watching the three tied men. She still had her Plant revolver out.

One of the deputy sheriffs hurried up and stared at the three men. "Ambrose, I told you last night to be careful today," the deputy said.

"You know these men?" Wendy asked.

21

The deputy looked at Canyon. "She's with me," the special agent said.

"Yep, know them. Don't really like them."

"Charge them with endangerment of a public official, Deputy. That should get them at least sixty days in the county jail. I don't want them lose when we come back through here next week."

"Who's gonna pay for my dead stallion?" the unhorsed man asked.

"You will, Wendell," the deputy said. "You're damn lucky the agent didn't fire at you instead of your horse." The deputy looked at Canyon. "You want me to take charge of them? I saw it all. I'll swear the complaint and be witness. Sheriff'll ask Judge Getts to give them at least ninety days for this and that'll cool them off a bit."

Canyon O'Grady nodded and he and Wendy watched as the deputy sheriff was joined by a second man with a star and they marched the three suspects off toward the jail.

The president had decided none of his talks would last more than five minutes. He was just finishing as Canyon and Wendy walked up the steps of the observation car.

President Buchanan waved at the cheering voters and then vanished into the rail car and hurried on through to his more secure one. Then Canyon and Wendy went in the observation car followed by the twenty troopers and their lieutenant.

The officer, Lieutenant Ken Ramstad, paused as his men filed into the coach and found seats.

"Nice work back there, O'Grady," Lieutenant Ramstad said.

Canyon nodded. "We happened to be in the right place at the right time. It can just as easy go the other way. We've got to be on top of everything, every minute."

"You can count on us, O'Grady."

"Good. This was a false alarm, but we don't know what is going to be at the next stop. Down the line somewhere I may want one or two of your best men. Have them designated. When I want them, I'll call to you, hold up one or two arms. Send me the one or two men on the double. I'll want your best shots, your men with the most combat experience with an enemy who shoots back."

"I have just the two men. I'll be ready for your signal."

Wendy and Canyon went to their area of the car nearest to the president's and looked at General Wheeler.

The general rubbed his left elbow. "I hit on that elbow when we went to the floor out there," he said. "I hope we don't have to do that every time."

"It was a good move, General. If those men had been aiming at the president, you would have saved his life. Now, where is our next stop?"

General Wheeler pointed to a map he had spread out on a makeshift table that had been arranged between two of the swing seats in the coach-style observation car.

"Right here, McClarren, Pennsylvania. It's another forty miles, just across the McClarren Bridge."

"Bridge? Every bridge could be a danger point. Is there a river there. How big is it? Do we have any report from the sheriff at McClarren?"

"The river is not big," Wendy said. "But it does go over a hundred-foot gorge."

"Do the locals have anyone guarding that bridge?" Canyon asked.

General Wheeler shook his head. "Canyon, we can't

have men guarding every mile of track. Somebody could topple a tree on the tracks at the last moment. Someone could burn up some ties and cause a derailment. A malcontent could park a heavy wagon loaded with black powder on some road crossing. We can't guard against every possible hazard on the seven hundred miles to Chicago and then seven hundred more back to Washington.''

Canyon dropped into a seat and nodded. ''I know it, General. I just wish that we could. I see so many ways that a man or a group of men who really wanted to hurt the president could do it.''

''I've been having nightmares about all of those possibilities since the president arranged this little trip two weeks ago,'' General Wheeler said. ''But he told me that we should take only reasonable and normal precautions. I first suggested two trains so any possible assassin wouldn't know which one he was on. But that wasn't approved. Then I wanted a company of soldiers, and he said no to that as well. We do the best we can under our restraints. That's all anyone can expect of us.''

As he sat there thinking it through, Canyon reloaded the cylinders of his army Colt percussion .44, which he had fired at the last stop. He loaded in the linen packages of powder and ball with the powder nearest the breach. Then he rammed the ball in, firmly sealing the cylinder to produce the total power of the powder. Last he applied percussion caps on the nipples of each newly loaded cylinder.

''He's right, Canyon,'' Wendy said from the next seat. ''All we can do is guard against the obvious and be there in case we're needed.''

Canyon lifted his brows but didn't reply. He slouched down in the seat. Maybe he could get an hour of sleep. A jabbering female agent was just what he needed on this assignment. For the life of him he still couldn't figure out why General Wheeler asked her to come along. He closed his eyes, but all he could see were more death traps for President James Buchanan.

Lea Jackson was the kind of person who did not leave the menial tasks to her helpers. She made sure everything was done correctly because she did it herself. She had selected the site—ten feet this side of where the railroad bridge began. She had dug out the hole under the heavy railroad tie and made it exactly the right size for fifty pounds of black powder.

Then she had ridden into the small town with the three men with her and they each bought twenty pounds of black powder, each from a different store. Then they were on the way out of the little settlement of McClarren.

They had ridden down from the railroad bridge to where the wagon road slanted down into the canyon and back up the other side to get into the town. Now they were ready with the black powder and burning fuse.

They had come into town singly and now were riding out the same way. They were just past the center of town when a man with a badge on came from the general store and called to Meckley, the first of the four who carried the sacks of black powder.

Meckley stopped in the street and the sheriff came up to him squinting against the sun.

"Hear tell you bought twenty pounds of black powder," the sheriff said. "Do I know you?"

"Don't rightly suspect. Name's Wilson, moved in five miles south along the river. I got me some stumps to blow out."

The sheriff nodded. "Yeah, I know how tough that can be. Wonder if you'd mind coming down and give me directions to your place. We're a bit touchy about black-powder sales hereabouts. Seems an important train is come along soon and we don't want nothing to happen to it.''

"Land sakes. Don't see how blowing stumps going to hurt any train.''

"Well, now, I know that, and you know that, but the important thing is that the attorney general of Pennsylvania don't know that. I've got instructions to hold until tomorrow any sales of black powder over a pound. Now, I know it's an inconvenience for you, but I got my orders.''

"Well, hell. Guess that means I got to spend the night in town. Sure as hell ain't riding home and back here tomorrow to get the powder.''

"Up to you, Mr. Wilson. Just hand down the powder and I'll give you a receipt and you can pick it up at my office tomorrow.''

Thirty yards behind Meckley, Lea Jackson saw her man stopped by the lawmen and she turned her horse in at a hitching rail and watched. When she saw the man with the bright silver star take the sack of black powder, she frowned, then left the rail and waved at her other two men who had been behind her and followed her pattern. They all rode out of town the other direction. They made it with no more encounters with the lawmen.

But now they had a time problem. The train was due to pass over the bridge at twelve-fifteen, just after noon. They still had sixty pounds of powder. That would be enough if they could get back to the bridge in time.

They made a wide circle around the town of Mc-Clarren. The time was slipping away. The damn sheriff had cost them at least an hour of extra riding time. Lea looked at the sun and kicked her horse into a gallop. They were still a mile from the gorge. They had to go down it, up the other side, get to the bridge, place the bomb, and at the same time hide the horses and conceal the man with the match who would light the fuse at the very last moment. They had less than an hour left.

Going down the steep trail into the gorge, Lea's horse hit a rock, stumbled, went down in front, and a foreleg snapped. The mount tried to stand on its front feet and bellowed with a scream of agony. The two men with Lea rode up, took her sack of black powder, and shot her horse, then lifted her to ride double and they hurried on down the slope and headed for the ford.

Lea swore like a teamster. "Dammit, Dickson. Can't you go any faster? We're running out of time."

Dickson, a short stocky man with more brawn than brainpower, shook his head. "I'm going as fast as I can without breaking another leg."

They crossed the stream and went up the other side, making better time on the up-slope. When they got to the top, they heard a train whistle.

"The damn train is early," Lea shouted. "Ride hard for the bridge. We only have three or four minutes."

She grabbed the third sack of black powder from her other man, Smith, and sent him out to the tracks as their lookout. When the train was in sight, he would signal them.

She and Dickson galloped the last quarter-mile to the tracks where they slanted across the bridge over the one-hundred-foot gorge.

Lea leapt off the horse, went to her knees with the shock of it, and shouted at Dickson. "Bring the other two sacks of powder, dammit! Run. We've got almost no time left."

They got to the edge of the bridge and the hole she

had dug out under one of the heavy, thick railroad ties. The blast would rip upward, snap the steel rail in half, and the train would not have time to stop. The engine would derail and slam over the next ten feet and into the gorge, dragging the president's cars with it, killing everyone on board.

She had one of the sacks of black powder pounded into place beneath the tie. Now she took the second one and rammed it in the space left. No room for the third one. She put it beside the others and cut off three lengths of the fuse.

Down the tracks she could hear the train whistle again at some crossing. Not much time!

"Dickson, can you see Smith down there?" she called.

Dickson looked and at last spotted the man beside the tracks three hundred yards away.

"Yeah, I see him, but I can't tell if his arms are up or down."

"Dammit, Smith! You shouldn't be down so far." She pushed the three lengths of fuse into the front sack of black powder. The first was a foot long, the second six inches, and the third three inches.

If this fuse burned a foot in sixty seconds as it was supposed to, she would be able to time the explosion to go off just before the engine hit this spot.

Dickson had been working at piling up a stack of trash and bush just in front of the spot where the bomb was so it would be hidden from the sharp eyes of the engineer on the train. If he saw someone near the tracks, he would stop the train and ruin the plan.

"Make the stack bigger," Lea shouted. She looked down the tracks. A cold sweat beaded her forehead. There it was! The big locomotive was coming. She could see the black spot of it, see the gushing black smoke. It was maybe a third of a mile away straight down the tracks, and coming fast. "Dickson, get out of here. Get back in the fringe of the trees. Take your horse with you. Quickly now!"

Lea lay down behind the pile of bush and saw that she could reach the fuses easily and not be seen downtrack. Once the fuse was lit, she would run like crazy down the sloping right-of-way and into the trees below. It didn't matter then if the engineer saw her or not. It would be far too late for him to stop the three-car train tearing along at the fantastic speed of thirty-five miles an hour.

She reached in the pocket of her denim pants for the block of stinker matches. They weren't there!

She tried the other pocket.

She didn't have the matches!

She lifted up and screamed. "Dickson! Do you have any matches?"

"No. Smith has them. He was the one who was supposed to light the fuse, remember?"

"Oh, damn!"

"Get off of there before they see you," Dickson yelled.

She searched her pockets again. They had planned it so carefully. Then it all fell through.

The train was still a quarter of a mile down the track. She lifted up and rolled down the sloping right of way. She scrambled to her feet, bent over, and ran for the brush and trees well below grade level.

She sat in the bushes near Dickson and let the tears stream down her face as the special train carrying the President of the United States barreled past.

Then the train was gone, over the bridge and slowing as it came into the town of McClarren.

Too late, the chance was gone. They would put the three packages of black powder in their suitcases and take the next train to the next town where the president was stopping—no, the second stop after this. That would give them plenty of time to plan it right. They wouldn't have a gorge like this one, but a train wreck would have to do. If the wreck didn't kill the bastard James Buchanan, they would charge into the upturned cars and finish the matter with sawed-off shotguns.

Lea Jackson hurried back to the tracks and pulled the fuses out of the black powder and then took the powder back to the horses.

Next time they would plan it with more care and allow more time. Next time they would not fail. She said a silent prayer for her dead father. Marsh Jackson had been the perfect father. They had just moved to the new farm when John Brown went on one of his rampages in Kansas and cut down her father one cold, snowy night with his short sword. Cut him down because he had favored the South and the right of Kansans to own slaves.

Lea Jackson would even the score. An eye for an eye, the Bible said. A life for a life. Her father was worth ten times as much as President James Buchanan, but she'd settle for him. A life for a life.

She lifted into the saddle.

"Let's go back in town and find Meckley and turn in these horses and get our train tickets. Should be a regular train through here in an hour or two."

3

Canyon O'Grady had been watching the McClarren Bridge as it came up on the track ahead. It appeared safe, well-made. Then the three-car train roared onto the wooden structure and Canyon held his breath for a moment as the timbers held and the train quickly rolled to the far side, where it started slowing down.

"McClarren just ahead," the special conductor on the president's train said. The conductor was the boss of the rolling equipment and was an absolute necessity on any train, the railroad people had explained before the run started. There was also one brakeman, one porter, an engineer, and a fireman. All five of the men were interviewed and someone from the attorney general's office checked their family backgrounds before they were selected to make this run with the president.

Canyon was at the door of the passenger car, which had an observation platform on the back. He watched the town slip past and the station come up. Two small boys ran along the right-of-way following the train. It used to be small boys ran after stagecoaches. Now it was trains. What would it be in another fifty years?

Canyon surveyed the entire scene—the street, the station, the platform, the crowd of people—watching for anything out of the ordinary, such as a canon trained on the president's car or a group of armed riders pacing the train. He saw nothing unusual.

The train rolled slower and slower until it came to a grinding stop at the small platform of the station in McClarren, Pennsylvania.

Canyon was the first one off the car. He ran lightly along the platform to the rear of the train and saw a pair of local lawmen holding a crowd of maybe two hundred people back from the train. They had roped off the area. Good.

He went under the rope, caught the glance of a sheriff's deputy, who nodded, and then Canyon began to circulate in the crowd. This whole trip was a bad idea. There was almost no chance to keep the president safe and hundreds of chances for someone to harm him. All Canyon could hope was that he could be in the right spot if anything else went wrong.

The soldiers came out smartly and surrounded the rear of the observation car. The people cheered. There were a few more now in the crowd, about three hundred Canyon estimated. There could be fifty revolvers and sawed-off shotguns in the crush of people and he would never know it until one of them killed the president. Dammit, he hated the chances the president took.

Canyon walked faster through the crowd, watching faces, looking for hatred and anger. He saw mostly smiles and cheering people. They crowded closer, but the guards and the ropes held them back thirty feet from the end of the observation car.

General Wheeler came out and welcomed the crowd, then presented the president. President James Buchanan strode out vigorously and waved at the cheering throng, then began his talk, the same one he had used before.

Canyon saw the woman too late. She was at the front of the crowd and quickly ducked under the rope and ran toward Buchanan. She held something in both hands, but Canyon couldn't tell what it was. Canyon charged forward. He pushed people aside, lifted the rope, and ran toward the woman. She was halfway across the open space. As Canyon ran, two of the riflemen advanced toward the woman, met her, and held their rifles out crossed in front of her so she could run no farther.

She carried a large bouquet of dried flowers in a fancy arrangement in a vase.

Canyon got there a moment later, took the flowers, held her arm, and marched her to the side of the crowd and under the rope.

"I only wanted to give the great man one of my dry-flower arrangements," the woman screeched. "I got a right to give President Buchanan a present."

Canyon examined the dry stems and weeds and pods and branches. It was artistic and pleasing, and there was no hidden pistol among them.

He handed the arrangement back to her. "Yes, ma'am, you certainly do. If you'll wait here, I'll see if the president has time to accept your flowers right after he speaks. You know why the soldiers stopped you?"

"No. All I have is my arrangement."

"But they didn't know that. There are some people who might try to hurt the president. We have to guard against that all the time. A pistol or a revolver could have been hidden in the bouquet."

Her eyes went wide. "Oh, my! I never thought of that. I hope I didn't—"

"No, you aren't in any trouble. If you wait here, I'll try to see that the president is told about your gift."

She nodded and Canyon went back to surveying the crowd. He saw at least eight deputy sheriffs and they seemed to be doing a good job. It all depended on the town. Twice he met Wendy Franklin, his special agent helper, watching the crowd as he was. It had been a damn-fool waste of time and money to bring her along on the trip. So far, she had been little help and he didn't see how she could be. But he was saddled with her for the next week. At least she was a pretty girl in a slender, blond kind of way.

He forgot her and looked at a man with baggy pants and wearing two old and ragged overcoats. It was cold, but not that cold. Canyon walked up to the man, who grinned.

"You with the president?" the man asked.

Canyon nodded and quickly patted his sides and his chest.

"I got no weapon. I won't hurt the president."

"Good, enjoy the talk." Canyon moved on. The chilly weather bothered him more than ever now. Most of the men wore long dusters or overcoats. Any one of them could have a rifle or full-sized shotgun hidden under there. But so far none had.

He saw Wendy again and motioned to her. She worked her way through the crowd to him.

"You saw the woman with the dry-flower arrangement?" Wendy nodded. "Go to the observation car and ask General Wheeler if the president would have time to accept the flowers from the woman. I think it would be a good thing for him to do."

"Right," Wendy said, and hurried toward the train.

Five minutes later it was all over. President Buchanan had waved at the cheering crowd and hurried back into the observation car, then on into his own converted private car. Several alterations had been made, including all but one of the windows being completely covered from the inside with sheets of quarter-inch steel plates.

The car was as safe as it could be made. It included

a full-sized bed in one end, a sofa, and several uphol-stered chairs that were fastened to the floor and a con-ference table with secured chairs as well.

The president had paused to accept the flowers from the woman, who had been so thrilled that she cried. It would be a story she would tell her grandchildren.

The train pulled slowly from the station at Mc-Clarren. They had been stopped exactly fifteen min-utes. Canyon tried to relax in the last car, but he couldn't. General Wheeler brought a message to him and let him read it.

"I don't understand, General," Canyon said.

Wendy had read it as well and she frowned.

"Simple. When we announced this trip, Senator Linden Paulson, of the new Republican party, told the Washington newspapers that he was going to follow the president. He would be a kind of 'truth squad' to set straight anything that the president said that was untrue or wrongly slanted. He said he'd follow us every mile of the way and stop and give a talk at the station wherever the president did.

"He tried it at Bixby, our first stop. He had been waiting there, I understand. By the time he started talking after we left, he had only ten people, and half of those drifted away. He told his friends it might not be worthwhile, after all. Then, when he looked at the train schedule, he realized that it would take him six to eight hours to get to each new spot where we spoke. The crowds would be gone long before that. The trains simply did not follow us around.

"The upshot of it all is that the senator went back to Washington and has given up his quest."

"Politically that is a win for the president," Canyon said. "I just hope that we can be as effective fending off any physical attacks on the nation's leader."

"Which means we need to review what we've done

so far." General Wheeler said. He favored his elbow that he had cracked when he pushed down the president at Bixby, and motioned for the other two to sit down at the makeshift conference table near the front of the railroad car.

"I'll bring Lieutenant Ramstad," Canyon said. "He might have some ideas for us." He walked up the aisle where the troopers and their commander sat, and brought back the young officer. He nodded.

"Lieutenant, sit down. We were just about to start a review of our first two stops and see if we need to change anything or if anyone has suggestions," General Wheeler said.

"So far we have had no actual attacks on the president. That's the way we like it. However, we have word that the Blue Goose Lodge looks at this trip as their best chance to get even with the president.

"Nobody argues that James Buchanan did a little middle-of-the-line marching when he was lining up delegates and proponents and supporters to gain the presidential nomination nearly five years ago now. He tried to walk a middle line so the southern delegates would look on him as the candidate most favorable to them. He did this by insisting that each state be allowed to handle the slavery question just as the states made their own laws about murder and prostitution and theft and land use and property taxes. He considered it a matter for state law, not federal.

"Now that's a moot point, at least in Kansas. The problem with Kansas is that they wanted the president to declare them a state by proclamation the way he is empowered to do in special circumstances. If he had done that while the southern supporters were in the majority, they could have a slave state.

"But he said the territory must qualify all of their officers before admission like the other territories. The

Kansas people hate him for that. As you know, the state qualified and voted to come into the union as a free state on January 29 of this year. The hard-liners down there are even more incensed now."

"So these Blue Goose Lodge people are going to be the ones we need to look out for the most?" Wendy asked.

"From everything we know," the general said. "Since the battle is over for the state, they might just fade away, but I doubt it. We have one report that the most bitter of the group have tattooed a small blue goose on the inside of their right wrist."

"We'll watch for it," Canyon said. "Where's the next stop?"

"Lawton, still in Pennsylvania."

"Do we need any changes?" Canyon asked. "Things seem to be working well so far."

"The president has asked to let the people come closer to the platform in back," General Wheeler said.

"They're within pistol range now, sir," Lieutenant Ramstad said. "We can't let them get any closer. I'd advise against it. In fact, if you want suggestions, I'd prefer my men to be out twenty yards and the people beyond that point another twenty yards to take them out of effective pistol range."

"I told the president we couldn't let the people any closer," General Wheeler said. "He's accepted it. I don't think he'd be pleased if we kept them back even farther. This whole trip is a little bit of back-patting for the president. He wants one more hurrah before he puts his presidential duties away."

"Let's hope it isn't a funeral procession we're guarding here," Canyon said. "I agree with you, General Wheeler. This is one train trip that never should have been made."

"Anything else we should change?" General Wheeler asked.

"I'm still worried about some object on the tracks that will cause a derailing and crash," Wendy said. "Is there anything we can do by talking to the railroad-management people?"

Canyon looked at her hoping his surprise didn't show on his face. "Right. The government wouldn't rent a second train for the trip. Maybe the railroad would want to contribute something?"

"Even a small locomotive engine running the track ten minutes before this one went over the route would be a help," Wendy said. "That would cut down the time anyone would have to damage the tracks or fall a tree over them before our train came past."

General Wheeler nodded. "The next time I talk to the railroad officials, I'll suggest that. Good idea."

That seemed to end the meeting. Canyon talked with the army officer for a moment, then the man went back to his troops.

Canyon and Wendy walked back to their seats. They had chosen seats on opposite sides of the car. She hesitated.

"I have a deck of cards. Would you like to play some two-handed whist?"

Canyon looked at her a moment. She was a well-formed young lady and she dressed so that was obvious. He shook his head. "Thanks, but I want to check over my weapons and be sure they're working right. Maybe later."

Wendy smiled a bit grimly and turned into her seat. She took a book from a small bag she carried, and began to read.

Canyon looked at her. He hoped they didn't have any real trouble. He intended to keep things as businesslike as possible. He admitted that he was still a little angry that General Wheeler had brought her along. He'd never worked with a woman before, especially a woman special agent. Damn-fool idea in the first place.

He settled down and stripped his percussion revolver and cleaned the parts, then put it back together again. He didn't disturb the five loads in the six-shot cylinder.

Wendy had glanced over at him once when he looked up. She quickly went back to her book.

Canyon took the Smith & Wesson #2 revolver from his inside belt holster. It sat high up under his arm and along his hip. It was only ten inches long, three inches shorter than his 1860 percussion. He liked the idea that it used solid loads and he could load it in the dark or in the rain and it would fire just as well.

Wet linen cartridges often didn't fire at all, or only with half-power. Canyon had heard about some gunsmiths who would bore straight through on the cylinder on a percussion pistol and convert it to fire solid cartridges. He didn't know if they made any for a .44. If they did, he could get them on special order through General Wheeler. He'd have to check on that. The slow pace of reloading the percussion revolver did have a lot of drawbacks.

He made a resolution to talk to a good gunsmith when he got back to Washington and find out about converting his percussion revolver.

Then he looked out the window as the countryside flashed by. They were going thirty-five miles an hour. Amazing! They were moving as far in two hours as he could ride in a hard sixteen-hour day on horseback. He just hoped the train wasn't rushing them into a spot that would be dangerous for the President of the United States.

4

Lea Jackson snarled at her two companions as they rode back into McClarren. She knew that the president's special train would be gone long before they could get to the station. She had been advised that they would stop for fifteen minutes only at any of the stations and then move on.

By the time she and Smith and Dickson rode back to the livery stable where they had rented the horses and saddles, the train station was empty. They found Meckley at the livery waiting for them. He was without the black powder but at least not in jail. Each had a carpetbag and they put the remaining three sacks of black powder in the bags and moved to the train station.

The next train toward Chicago wouldn't be through for a half-hour. They ate a quick meal at a nearby café and waited.

Lea was twenty-six years old and only two inches over five feet, so she had to look up at the three men she traveled with. Even so, they knew who was the boss and who cracked the whip.

She shook her straight black hair that had been cut short so she looked a little mannish from the back of her head. But she liked her hair that way, since it was simple to take care of. She drummed her fingers on the bench outside the station as she waited for the train.

The next time she would have everything right. Every one of them would have matches and fuse. They all would know each step in case one man went down. Next time she would kill President James Buchanan.

She had the plans worked out. The next stop for the president was Lawton, Pennsylvania, about thirty miles east. Since they were now behind the president's train, they had to skip the next three stops and be ready for him at Junction City. That way their train would pass the president's on a siding somewhere along those next three stops.

Then they would go with plan two, rifles. More sure, but with more danger to the assassins. The three men she had brought with her were expert snipers, marksmen of the first caliber. It all depended how close they could get to the target. That was the next step.

Lea studied her men as she waited. Meckley was the best of the three. He came from Georgia, had actually gone to a year of college before he came to Kansas from Missouri to help out in the cause. He was almost six feet tall, had dark black hair, and could speak with a precise Kansas drawl that left her surprised. His usual voice was full of dripping southern molasses.

She had crumbled the first time she met him, and they had made wonderful love all night. He was steady and sure of himself. If war came, as he was sure it would, he had a commission already promised as a captain in the Georgia First Volunteers.

Dickson was the strongest man in the group, but sometimes a little slow mentally. He was also the best shot in the team. She was counting on him for Junction City. That would end it. The four of them would then split up and make their way by train or stagecoach back home to Kansas. Dickson was thick in the shoulders, with arms like railroad ties and legs that bulged his pant legs sometimes.

Smith was one she hadn't wanted to bring, but Dickson wouldn't leave without him. He was thin and sallow-skinned, sickly-looking beside the other two, but he said he could shoot and he knew black powder. Now she wasn't so sure about him. But he was on the strike, so he stayed.

They had bought tickets individually at different times and sat or stood apart on the small station platform. Nobody could report a group of four persons leaving McClarren this day.

Lea heard the train whistle. The huffer should be here soon. She moved a wide silver bracelet on her right wrist and stared at her source of strength. There she had tattooed a picture of a standing blue goose. He was an inch and a half high. She stroked the picture tenderly, then covered it with the bracelet and stood with her heavy bag, looking down the tracks with the others who were waiting.

Canyon O'Grady had been watching the countryside for twenty minutes when General Wheeler came and stood in the aisle. When Canyon looked up, the general motioned to him and to Wendy, who watched him.

"The two of you need to meet the rest of the president's entourage. He likes to have some of his advisers with him. The three men you'll meet are all highly regarded by the president. None of them has cabinet status, but they help and assist and do have considerable power in the administration.

"Come down this way and we'll get the formalities over. I think it would be good to have one of them, a man named Ambrose Galbreath, to sit in on our planning sessions, such as they are. We may need an outside viewpoint."

General Wheeler led them through the car, into the

narrow slot between the rail cars, over the gently moving coupling plate, and into the president's private car.

It recently had been made available to the president to use whenever he needed rail travel.

They had been there before, but now there were three men they had not met. They stood when Wendy came in, and General Wheeler made the introductions.

The first was Galbreath, a hulking man of six feet, two inches, heavily built with a growing paunch, but not much fat. He was in his fifties, Canyon decided, and had bushy eyebrows over piercing blue orbs, and a heavy shock of hair just starting to gray.

The second one was Maurice Hinchliff, a balding skeleton of a man. His brown suit hung on him like it would on a stick figure. He had deep-set pale-brown eyes, a large nose, and a chin that quivered most of the time. His handshake was firm and honest and Canyon liked him at once. He was probably about sixty.

Hinchliff grinned at Canyon. "So this is that miracle man who's been saving our scalps out West? Glad to meet you, young man."

"I'm glad to be here and meet you, Mr. Hinchliff," Canyon said.

The last man was called Bill Thibadeau and he was somber, with brown hair combed forward and to the side to cover up a bald spot. He shook his head as he took Canyon's hand.

"Don't know how I got dragged along on this little parade. Told Jim not to come. But you know him once he gets his teeth into a damn idea."

The president laughed with affection. "Thought you field operators should meet my White House team. I know they're a mangy lot, a ragtag bunch, but they're all I've got. These are the toughest ones left of my Old Men of the Night, that shadow cabinet the press accused me of having. Claimed we met at night so no one would know.

"Hell, we met at night so these gents could get away from their wives and we could have a good old-fashioned poker party."

They all laughed.

The president waved a steel-nubbed pen at the three. "Canyon is my head of security for this run. I hope that if he asks one of you to do something, you'll comply at once. He knows what he's doing. Saw him with his shirt off once. He's got more bullet scars than you'd want to count. He must have some practical sense to get shot that many times and still be alive."

"Or maybe I simply don't know how to dodge." Canyon threw in.

They laughed again.

"General Wheeler thought it might be good to have one of you in on our review and planning sessions. Mr. Galbreath, would you honor us with your presence? The defense team gets together right after the next stop and hash it over."

"I'd be delighted," Galbreath said.

The porter came in with coffee and they waited until he had served it in sturdy railroad cups and left.

"So far, so good," President Buchanan said. "I told the three of you that you were jousting at devils that weren't even there."

"I couldn't be happier," Canyon said. "But, Mr. President, we have a lot of rails to cover before we have you safely back in Washington a week from today."

"We'll do it, Canyon. You see, I've become somewhat of a philosopher in my last month in office. My logic tells me that I'm not the right kind of president to be a martyr. Not enough flash, not enough compassion with the people. I don't mix well enough.

Ergo, I will not be killed on this trip. It's all a matter of simple logic.''

The conductor knocked and then opened the door from the far end of the president's car.

"Lawton in ten minutes, Mr. President," he said, grinned, and walked out again.

"Time to get the show ready," General Wheeler said. "We'll have another evaluation right after this stop. We'll be in the next car. You're welcome to join us, Mr. Galbreath."

Canyon and Wendy went back to their posts.

The stop at Lawton went smoothly. There were only about fifty people there for the speech. There were three extra deputy sheriffs on horseback and the crowd was polite and cheered for the president.

At Spring Shore, still in Pennsylvania, the crowd was much larger, but there were fifteen sheriff's deputies to help maintain order. More than six hundred sat on roofs and crowded into the street and overflowed on both sides of the tracks.

Canyon rushed forward into the crowd only once when what seemed like shots sounded at the far edge of the crowd and some people laughed. When he got there, he found it was only two small boys with firecrackers. They had saved them from the Fourth of July to set off in the snow.

The evaluation after the Spring Shore stop was quick. Ambrose Galbreath said he thought it went well.

"The president is a little smoother now, seems more casual when he gives the same speech. After six or eight more times he should have it down well."

They chuckled.

"We made it through another one," General Wheeler said. "The toughest one so far is coming up. It's at Junction City, the largest town we've stopped at yet. I telegraphed ahead and asked for the Pennsylvania state militia to turn out fifty to a hundred troops to help control the crowd.

"The sheriff there predicted that we would have two thousand people crowding around the train. That's a place where we could find some real trouble. Let's everyone be on our guard."

"We still planning on laying over during the night and start again in the morning?" Galbreath asked.

"Yes, that was in the original plans," the general said. "I don't see any reason to change those plans. Does anyone else?"

"It means more stops," Canyon said. "If I had a vote, I'd say we wrap up the last speech with nightfall and highball it straight into Chicago during the night."

General Wheeler nodded. "Me too. Unfortunately, neither one of us gets a vote."

They came into Junction City just before noon. They were a hundred and seventy miles from Washington, but still more than five hundred from Chicago.

Canyon hung out the side of the car from the steps watching the train creep into the station. There seemed to be people everywhere. Mounted deputies were herding the crowd off the tracks where the train had to roll.

Dozens of people lined the rails on both sides for a block before the station. As soon as the three cars passed, the people surged onto the tracks and ran after the train.

This could be trouble, Canyon decided. He checked both his weapons, then swung down from the car as it came up to the start of the platform.

A deputy ran up and Canyon asked him how many men the sheriff had patrolling and controlling the crowd.

"Twenty men, ten mounted sir. Are you with the president?"

"Yes. Did the militia arrive?"

"A company, about sixty, sir. They're waiting orders."

The train stopped. Canyon and the deputy walked toward the end platform. The crowd surged around them.

"Go bring twenty of the militia with an officer to the rear of the train, now," Canyon barked.

The deputy almost saluted as he turned and ran through the thickening crowd.

Lieutenant Ramstad brought his troops out on a double-time trot and tried to take their regular positions, but people already had pressed against the very edge of the observation platform.

"Push them back," Canyon called, and the lieutenant ordered his men to fix their bayonets and then slowly they forced the crowd back about twenty feet. The soldiers stood there with their bayonets facing directly forward, forming a steel fence around the end of the car.

The militia came promptly, surging through the side of the crowd. They had on some semblance of a uniform. Canyon ordered a row of them to stand directly behind the regular troops around the car, and the rest of them to position along the platform side of the rest of the train.

A moment later General Wheeler came out and held up his hands for quiet. It took two or three minutes for the chatter and talk to quiet.

"Good afternoon. It's fine to see so many of you." People stood on wagons, sat on horseback, hung out windows and some perched in trees and on the roofs of buildings.

Canyon figured there were at least three thousand people jammed into the area around the station.

"Now, here's the man you came to see, the President of the United States!"

Wild cheering filled the area; the clapping and shouting went on for two minutes after President James Buchanan stepped up to the heavy, shielded lectern.

Canyon moved back from the soldiers, working his way through the densely packed crowd. He wanted to get to the back as he always did. This time if he went to the back of the audience he might be a hundred yards away.

He settled for a spot where the crowd thinned about forty yards back from the president. There were too many people, they were too close to the president, and there wasn't a way in the world that they could offer adequate protection to the nation's leader.

The president was nearly done with his five-minute talk when Canyon heard the crack of a high-powered rifle shot. His head turned in the direction of the sound. He heard some screams. Then spotted a puff of blue smoke coming from the roof of a small store across the street from the station not more than sixty yards from the president.

Shooting fish in a barrel range! Canyon drove through the crowd. Someone screamed. He looked back at the lectern. The president had dropped below it just as a second shot slammed toward him.

General Wheeler had lunged toward the president, and this time the heavy rifle slug caught the general high in the arm and spun him around and slammed him backward to the side of the car, where he slumped to the floor.

Six of the riflemen in front of the observation platform leapt on the open area, shielding the president, their rifles up, with orders to shoot at anyone firing. They had no target. The blue smoke over the one-story building roof had dissipated quickly in a light wind.

Canyon bulled past the last of the crowd and sprinted for the alley behind the store. It would have no ceiling access door. Probably a wooden ladder up the back of the building.

By the time Canyon rounded the corner of the alley he saw two men dropping off the ladder on a building about thirty yards down. He yelled at them, and one turned and fired a rifle at him. Canyon had his .44 in hand. He stopped, aimed, and pulled the trigger. The man who had shot took a round in the thigh but kept on running.

Canyon sprinted after them. One of the men ahead fired to the rear as he ran, but it was an unaimed shot that missed. Canyon gained on them before they got to the first corner. He saw both men jump on horses and head down the street. He was within twenty-five yards of the men now and fired at the closest one four times with the big 1860 percussion. One of the rounds hit the rider in the side. The bullet drove upward and plunged into his heart, stopping the big blood pump in midstroke.

The rider collapsed on the saddle and fell off on the far side as both horses galloped down the street.

Canyon looked around for a horse, but there was not a one along the block of hitching rails. By the time he ran to the main street and found one, the horseman would be out of sight. He had no time to track the man.

Two sheriff deputies ran up and Canyon pointed to the dead man and told them to take care of him. Find out who he was and if he was from around there.

Canyon started to leave, then ran to the dead man and looked at his right wrist. He pushed back a blue shirt sleeve and saw what he was afraid he would, a tattoo of a blue goose.

Back at the train, Lieutenant Ramstad and two of

his men had shielded the president as he scurried into the last coach and then quickly into his protected railroad car.

General Wheeler crawled into the first car and held a hankerchief over the backside of his arm where the rifle slug had drilled through. It had taken out an inch of flesh when it exited.

One of the troopers hurried in with a shoulder bag filled with medical supplies. "General, I'm the sawbones for our outfit. Corporal Braun. If it's all right with the general, I could do a quick bandage there and stop the bleeding. One of our men went for a local doctor to treat you properly."

"Yes, Corporal Braun. That's a good idea. I didn't know that our troops had men trained in minor surgery this way."

"Most companies don't, sir. But we thought there might be some need and we weren't authorized to bring an army surgeon."

Corporal Braun removed the general's uniform jacket, rolled up the sleeve of his shirt, and cleaned the wound, then put on a compress and wrapped it with an inch-wide roll of cloth the corporal had torn out of white sheets he had bought himself.

"Doesn't look like it hit the bone, sir."

"Good. Do you know if they got the sniper?"

"Not sure. We had some men go after him. Just one rifle fired, from what I understand."

"The president wasn't hurt, was he?"

"No, sir, I don't think so. I saw him walking through the car when I came in."

Canyon O'Grady rushed into the coach and saw the corporal finishing his bandaging. "Was the president hurt?" Canyon asked.

"No, we don't think so. Only two shots. I made the mistake of trying to catch the second one. Let's get the train moving as quickly as we can. You tell the crowd. Check to be sure President Buchanan is not hurt.''

Canyon knocked on the president's car door and Ambrose Galbreath answered it.

"Is the president unhurt?" Canyon asked.

"Yes, just a little shaken and disappointed."

"Tell him we'll be moving as soon as we can get the tracks cleared."

Outside, Canyon told the militia captain to use his men to clear the tracks of pedestrians in front of the train. He ran to the engineer and told him they would leave as soon as the tracks were clear. The man nodded, blew his whistle, and gushed steam out from the engine in clear warning to the people who backed away from the roaring, screaming steam engine.

Canyon went to the observation platform. He held up his hands for quiet, then he shouted to the crowd. "The president has not been harmed. We must move on. He is sorry he couldn't finish his remarks to you. One of the men who tried to hurt the president has been captured. Please now back away from the train so we can get under way."

People cheered when he waved, and the crowd began to break up and people drifted off.

The sheriff ran up and waved at Canyon. He was a small man with a homburg and no gun.

Canyon met him at the train steps.

"Sir, I am Joshua Kincaid, county sheriff. I understand you or one of your security men killed one of the snipers. Is that right?"

"Yes. I did. My name is Canyon O'Grady. I'm a special agent of the United States government. I'll write out a statement and mail it to you. Will that be enough? It was a death by a law officer in the line of duty."

"That should be fine, Mr. O'Grady. I'm sorry to say the others got away. There were at least three more of them we saw. They rode away on horses and we had no way to track them. My men aren't very good at that anyway. With all of these people leaving the tracks are now wiped out."

"At least the president wasn't harmed. Thanks for your help."

The train pulled out a few minutes later. A civilian doctor had hurried on board, looked at the general's wound, and wrapped it back up. "The soldier did as good a job as I could," he said, and stepped off the train just before it left the station.

Canyon O'Grady was glad to get away from Junction City.

5

The evaluation after Junction City was sharp and angry. General Wheeler insisted on being there. He was still hurting. The doctor had given him some laudanum for the pain and they wanted to get the talk done before the general faded into his opium-induced painless time.

"I think we should insist that the president make no more stops on the way to Chicago," Canyon said. "He's taking unnecessary chances, risks that he shouldn't be. He must be told."

"It's like talking to a brick wall," Ambrose Galbreath said. "General Wheeler, you were there when we had the first argument. He wants to do this and I don't think one gunshot is going to deter him."

"We need something as tough as steel that you can see through," Wendy said. "We should surround him with it when he's back there talking. Canyon is right. We've got to advise him not to make any more appearances."

"We're scheduled for stops at a dozen more places," Galbreath said. "The newspapers have been printing the story for days. A lot of people would be disappointed."

"They'll be sad, too, when the president is shot dead," Canyon said.

Lieutenant Ramstad nodded. "I agree with you. We

have to advise him not to go on the platform anymore. I just don't have enough men here to protect him.''

"Just which of you heroes is going to go in there and tell him he can't go to the podium anymore?'' General Wheeler asked. He sighed. The laudanum was starting to work. ''All right, all right. Make it unanimous. I agree he shouldn't go out there again, but we've got another stop scheduled in about an hour. I'm not going to be doing much by then. Damn arm hurts like crazy.''

"We all should go see him,'' Canyon said. ''I'll talk if you want me to.''

"At least the Blue Goose Lodge members are behind us now,'' Lieutenant Ramstad said.

"Maybe not for long,'' Canyon said. ''You've seen sometimes we're on a siding at a town and another train will come in from behind us and take on passengers and move on past us? It could take the Blue Goose men two or three stops so they can get ahead of us on a regularly scheduled train if they try.''

"Count on it,'' Wendy said.

"Damn,'' General Wheeler barked.

"We know we're going to lose our argument with the president,'' Canyon said. ''He's the boss. So are we going to suggest that he cut back or put restrictions on what he does?''

"We should wire ahead to the next stops requesting the sheriff to ask for at least fifty militia be on hand as an honor guard who can also help maintain order,'' Lieutenant Ramstad said. ''That's part of the militia's job.''

"Good idea,'' Canyon said. ''Lieutenant, you get that done at the next stop.''

"We could put some sides on that podium,'' Wendy suggested. ''If somebody had a gun on either side of the platform, President Buchanan'd be an easy target.''

"Good," Canyon said. "Wendy, you talk to the conductor, see what we can get on board, and if nothing is here, make it his job to get some steel-plated protection on both sides of the podium. That will help. You follow up on him."

She left at once to talk to the conductor.

Canyon looked at General Wheeler. The army man was smiling, nodding, as if singing a little song. They helped him into a back seat that had been turned into a small bed, and helped him stretch out.

Then Canyon, Lieutenant Ramstad, and Ambrose Galbreath went in to see the president.

It was a quick meeting. Canyon presented the recommendation of the defense committee. Buchanan listened patiently, said he understood the dangers, had accepted them, but wanted to stop at as many of the scheduled towns as possible. He thanked them.

"Now to the important things. How is Rufus' arm? He was really hurting when I talked to him a few minutes ago. Did that doctor come and did he get some laudanum?"

They told him that the general was feeling no pain now and was sleeping.

Back in the last car of the train the three men shrugged.

"We tried," Galbreath said.

"I wonder if anyone will remember that during the state funeral for our dead president?" Canyon asked. "The bunch that hit us in Junction City can't touch us for two or three stops. But for all we know, they may have four or five teams of assassins along this stretch of track. They could hit us anywhere, at any time. That includes while we're moving. Has the engineer been instructed to watch for problems on the tracks?"

Galbreath nodded. "I heard General Wheeler talk to him about that very subject."

"This is a nightmare," Canyon fumed. "The president's schedule has been sent out so they can draw crowds. That means every person who has ever wanted to kill our president knows where he'll be and the exact time. President Buchanan has only one more month in office. Why not let him serve it out in peace?"

"Hatred can run deep in the human soul," Galbreath said. "I guess those of us who don't have that kind of emotion just can't understand it."

Canyon walked up the aisle and back down. "Galbreath, you're probably right. But I have one more stopgap we might be able to do. At the next station I'm going to drop off an order to telegraph the next ten stations where we stop and have the sheriffs there pick up for questioning and jail any suspicious characters who might harm the president.

"That could be people who have made threats, or do dangerous things, who buy black powder, large amounts of weapons, anything like that. We might just catch a prize fish or two in a net that way."

Canyon walked past General Wheeler. The old army man lifted up and motioned to him. "Boy, you'll have to stand on the podium, introduce the president. Anybody shoots, you get between them and the president, promise?"

"Yes, yes, now you relax. We'll take care of everything. The president asked about you. Just have a good rest and a few wild dreams and we'll talk to you in the morning."

"Try. Wild dreams. I've been sleeping and waking. Arm don't hurt. Damn good old laudanum." He closed his eyes and was sleeping again.

The next three stops went like clockwork. They were mostly at smaller towns and there were no firecrackers or charging horses. They were on the third stop now

56

since the shooting, and Wendy paced behind the hundred-odd people listening to Buchanan.

A man came from behind a small group of people and she saw that he carried a rifle. She angled toward him, then ran. The man looked her way curiously, then turned away. Wendy had out her revolver and covered him before he could take more than a few paces.

"Take another step and you're a dead man," Wendy spat at him in a cold steady voice.

The man stopped and turned. The rifle was in both hands, like a soldier carries one when he runs. His eyes went wide.

"What. . . . what's going on? Why the gun?"

"Let go of the rifle with your left hand and then bend down and lay it on the ground," Wendy ordered.

He did so slowly, making no sudden moves. Then he stood up. "Now, tell me what the hell is going on. I just got back to town from a three-day ride downstate and I see this big bunch of people. We got a hanging or something?"

"You don't know?"

"Not an idea."

"You didn't know that nobody was supposed to carry a gun in this part of town today?"

" 'Course not. I've been out of town for three days."

A deputy sheriff in his uniform shirt walked up grinning.

"Looks like she caught you dead to rights, Leon," the deputy said.

"George, what the hell—"

Wendy looked at the lawman. "Deputy, you know this man?"

"Yes, ma'am. He's Leon, my brother-in-law. A farmer lives downstate a piece."

"Then tell him to take his rifle, leave the hammer down, and take it home before I confiscate it."

"Yes, ma'am, I'll surely do that." The deputy picked up the rifle and tossed it to the other man. "Come on, Leon, you heard what the lady government agent said."

Wendy watched them until the man with the rifle was out of sight behind a building. Then she turned back, grinned, and kept walking through the crowd around the back of the train as the president finished his talk.

Back on the train after they left town, they all relaxed a little.

"No problems in three straight stops," Wendy said. "Maybe it's a good omen."

"Or maybe we're running out of good luck," Canyon said. "It may be that we have only one band of Blue Goose Lodge folks to worry about. It used to be four in the bunch, now it's three. We're in the area where they could strike again."

Canyon looked at the army officer. "Ramstad, I want you to have your men keep their weapons loaded at all times. I want them ready to respond to shots fired at this train within five seconds. That means they'll have to know how to open the windows. If they can get them up from the bottom, it will be best then they'll have protection. You might want to give them some basic training on raising the windows."

Ramstad left to talk to his men.

"I hear you stopped a man with a rifle back there, Wendy," Canyon said.

"Yes. He just got into town, no threat."

"Still, he could have been. Good work."

Wendy grinned. "Well, thanks. A kind word now and then helps out a lot."

Canyon laughed and headed for his seat. It was turning out better than he expected, working with a woman agent.

Lea and her two men found exactly the right spot. It was where a patch of woods grew to within twenty feet of each side of the right-of-way and the tracks were almost at grade level. They dug a hole for the three twenty-pound sacks of black powder under a wooden tie. This time they had a short shovel they had bought in town to make the digging faster.

They were somewhere in the country, with nobody around to notice them. The wagon road along here was almost a mile from the railroad tracks. The time was nearing six, and it was so dark they couldn't see one another ten feet away.

They had checked the schedule of the president's train at the last depot. He wasn't set to stop there, but the train would be through there at five-forty. The stationmaster said he had to know that so he could keep the local train heading for Chicago on the siding while the special went through.

So the only train that would be going this way after five-forty would be the president's train.

Lea packed the powder into the hole and put a big rock against the three bags, then piled dirt up on the outside, leaving only one small place, where she had rammed in a foot-long fuse. There would be no hurry this time. She would time the train and light the fuse for a one-minute burn.

No one would see her or the fuse. That would give her plenty of time to get back to the woods.

As she finished packing the dirt around the tie, she remembered that terrible day when John Brown had left a trail of death through Kansas.

She had been with her mother in that small cabin near the creek. John Brown had come to the door with his five sons well after dark and asked her pa to come outside. John Brown said he had an ailing horse. Her father was good with animals.

Marsh Jackson pulled on a coat and went outside to consider the sick horse.

Before he could get his eyes accustomed to the dark, one of the boys hit him with his big fist against his shoulder and drove him down to his knees.

"Why the hell you hit me, boy?" Marsh yelled.

John Brown came up to Marsh Jackson and laughed. "The boy just having some fun. He didn't mean no harm." Brown looked at Marsh in the spill light from the cabin window. "You fancy wanting to make Kansas a free state or slave?" Brown asked.

"Don't matter much to me one way or tother," Marsh Jackson said.

"Don't, huh? We hear different. Let's say you had to decide. Which way would you vote, Marsh Jackson? Then what would you say?"

"Dang it, I come from Tennessee. Guess I'd have to favor the South and the slave vote."

"Just wanted to know, Marsh, just wanted to know. Now, we need you to come down the road a piece to see that horse."

"Let me get my boots on. All I got are these inside slippers. Figured the animal was right close."

"Won't matter none," one of the boys said.

One of the big men caught Marsh Jackson by an arm and they walked him down the snow-covered road a hundred yards.

"Far enough, Pa?" one of the boys asked.

"Hell, yes," John Brown said.

The boys let go of Marsh and John Brown leaped forward and struck Marsh Jackson in the neck with a heavy eighteen-inch sword. Marsh went to his knees, bleeding severely. He cried out once, then the boys

60

used their heavy swords, hacking at him, splitting his head open, lopping off one arm and slashing his chest.

When the savage chopping finished, Marsh lay on the ground dead of multiple wounds.

John Brown took out a revolver, put the muzzle at the back of Marsh Jackson's head, and fired one shot.

Lea had been waiting in the cabin for her pa to come back. When she heard him leave with the men she had been afraid. Her ma said it would be all right. Then the time stretched out.

When Lea heard the shot, she screamed and knew that her father was dead. She caught up a rifle and rushed outside, but the five horses and the five men were gone. She screamed at them that they would pay for such a dastardly murder, then she fired the old rifle in the direction they had taken, and screamed again.

Lea sat in the light skiff of snow beside the tracks, waiting. The train should be coming anytime now. She took out the plug of wax-bound matches and lit one for practice. She used a rock and the match struck the first time. She put it out quickly. Lea could hear the men moving around in the brush. They were not as dedicated as she was.

She would avenge her father's death a dozen times over if she could. An eye for an eye, a life for a life.

She put her hand on the tracks and could hear them humming.

"Coming," she said, and the men heard her and settled down, their rifles loaded, their revolvers ready with six chambers filled.

Two minutes later she could hear the growling of the big engine. Then, far down the straightaway she could see a pinpoint of light that would be the three feeble lanterns on the train engine. She caught the fuse so she knew where it was in the dark, then she held two torn-off matches ready. She lay them against the rock set to strike them.

The train came closer.

Again and again she heard that revolver shot in the darkness. Again and again she saw the remains of her poor father the next morning staining the snow red with his blood.

Now she could hear the whistle of the train as it blew for some road crossing. Less than a mile away. She used her knife and cut the fuse in half. A thirty-second fuse. Yes, better. She could estimate how far the train would travel in thirty seconds. Better to be a little early than late.

The lights were brighter on the front now. The sound of the train was easy to hear. She waited.

"Light the damn thing," Meckley called from the woods.

She hesitated, then scratched the match. It didn't light. She scratched it the second time and it flared into flame. She cupped it with her hand and touched the burning brand to the powder-laden fuse. It caught and began to sputter as it burned.

Lea leapt up and ran for the woods. She fell down, got up, and ran again as the train barreled down the tracks toward her.

The train was closer than she figured. Then it was upon them, huffing and grinding and steaming and roaring as it swept past them. Just as the last car cleared the bomb, the woods lit up with the blast of sixty pounds of black powder as it exploded. The force of the blast sent a shock wave of wind whipping into the woods, causing Lea to suck in a breath.

The tie over the bomb blasted upward, ripping the track and six ties with it and breaking the connection between the steel rails at the joint.

The flash and roar of the explosion rumbled and echoed down the tracks both ways.

Lea sat there in the woods with leaves and dirt blasted into her face, but she didn't bother to brush them away. She cried, bawled like a wounded child. The blast had been two or three seconds too slow. If the match had lit that first try . . .

Lea let out a long wail of frustration and defeat and began pounding on the ground with her fists.

Meckley came up to her, pulled her into his arms, and held her until the rage went away.

He took over for a moment. "Now we have to ride to the next town. Didn't you say the train would spend the rest of the night there? Yes, it's Oakville, Ohio, and we're no more than five miles from there. We'll get these nags moving and be there in plenty of time for a good dinner and a hotel room. We can get the train out before the president leaves in the morning, and set up our next ambush down the line. Come on, we've got to move. No time to waste."

Lea let them help her on her horse and followed. Tonight it was good to have somebody to take the lead for a while. By the time they got to Oakville she would have a new plan worked out, one that would be better than the others.

Canyon O'Grady had been looking out the back of the coach car when the blast went off. He had felt the shock wave hit the train as well as some small rocks. The blast lit up the sky for a few seconds, then faded.

"What the hell?" a soldier yelled.

"A bomb, a big one on the tracks," Canyon answered. "We got past it by about a second. If that had come five seconds earlier, it would have tumbled all of this train off the tracks."

Wendy ran up to him in the aisle and touched his

shoulder. "That would have been tragic," she said. "But it looks like our luck is still holding."

"Not luck at all," Canyon said grimly. "The person who lit the fuse simply timed it wrong. Sometimes fuse will burn twice as fast as it's supposed to. Then again, some days it burns twice as slow as it should. Black powder is hard to work with."

"I'm glad we're stopping in Oakville," Wendy said. "Does that mean we get to have a real bed in a hotel?"

"It's in the budget," Canyon said. "I might stay on board. We'll have half of the soldiers on guard duty around the train in the rail yard. That means a siding. Anyone could get to the train while it's stopped."

"It would be better for you if you had a good night's rest," Wendy said. Then she looked away.

Canyon let out a long sigh. "You're right. I'll try to find a hotel room."

"Nothing will go wrong tonight," Wendy said. "I have one of my feelings about this."

Canyon laughed. "I'm going to the hotel anyway," he said.

6

When they arrived at Oakville that evening, Canyon made sure the train was on a siding and secured with ten soldiers guarding it. They would be rotated every two hours. Then he found the stationmaster and talked to him for fifteen minutes.

"Best suggestion I'd have is to use old Engine Three-eight-five out there. She's fit and ready to go. All I'll need is an approval from Chicago to do it."

They worded the telegram together and sent it to four of the top officers in the rail line in Chicago.

> Hereby urgently request that Engine 385 now available in Oakville, Ohio, be released to sweep the tracks from here to Chicago when the President of the United States continues his trip tomorrow at 8:30. This urgent request is for the safety of the president. Two incidents have occurred already. Please rush approval to stationmaster, Oakville, Ohio.
>
> Major General R. W. Wheeler,
Chief of Staff,
White House, Washington D.C.

The stationmaster looked up and nodded. "Damn well should do it. I'll go ahead and get Three-eight-five ready. The engineer will be instructed to leave ten minutes before you do, and stay within ten minutes of your train at all times."

"What's our chances of approval from Chicago?" Canyon asked.

"I'd say ninety-nine out of a hundred. Sleep easy, Mr. O'Grady."

Sleep. Not a major item. He checked the train again. One of the soldiers with a bayonet-fixed rifle challenged him within three steps.

Canyon congratulated the soldier and walked two blocks to the hotel, where a room waited for him. He went to the desk in the lobby and got his key.

"Yes, Mr. O'Grady, that's Room Twenty-four front. Have a good sleep." The room clerk handed him the key and smiled.

As he turned, a woman stepped forward. She was small and a little thick at the waist with short dark hair and a curious smile.

"So you're the famous Canyon O'Grady," she said. She held out her hand. "Hi, I'm Lea Jackson with the *Kansas City Blade*. I finally caught up with you. My editor told me to follow the train and do human-interest stories."

"Yes, Miss Jackson. Good evening. I'm sorry, I just have no story for you. There are lots of good items for you here, but I'm not the source. I wish you well but I really need to get some sleep. It's been a long day."

"I know! I understand you left Washington, D.C., very early this morning and made eight or nine stops. Amazing."

Canyon began walking toward his room with a small overnight bag.

She kept up with him. "It wouldn't take much time, a half hour," she said. "I have a lot of readers who wonder about the man who's chief of security on the president's special train. You're responsible for keeping the president safe, I'd guess."

"Yes, that's about right. I wish you well on your

story." Canyon strode off quickly, leaving her behind. He went up the steps to the second floor and into his room. He turned the key in the lock and heaved a big sigh. So far, so good.

He had just stripped off his shirt when a knock sounded on the door. Canyon closed his eyes for a moment and took a deep breath and went to the door. "Who is it?"

"Mr. O'Grady, there's a man here with a telegram. He said it was important."

"Miss Jackson?"

"Yes. I saw him looking for your room and . . ."

A telegram. It could be a reply from Chicago. Early, but telegrams went fast. He pulled the door open. Quicker than he expected, Lea Jackson pushed the door open more and scooted under his arm into his room.

"Miss Jackson!"

"Now don't be mad, Canyon. You're an amazingly attractive man and you can't blame a girl for trying. I get my stories any way I can."

"No telegram?"

"No telegram. Wasn't I naughty?" She took off the jacket she wore and quickly unbuttoned her soft white blouse.

Canyon shook his head. "Look, you're a pretty girl and nice, but I just don't have the time—"

The blouse fell off her shoulders and to the floor. She stood there bare to the waist. Her breasts swung from the motion. They were full, with heavy rose areolae centered by large nipples already starting to enlarge and fill with hot blood.

She walked to him and looked up. "Sometimes, Canyon, a woman sees a man she wants, and she doesn't mind doing the asking. Like now, Canyon. Am I so ugly you don't want me?"

Hot blood pounded in his groin, he couldn't take his

gaze from her beautiful breasts. She caught his hands and lifted them to her breasts and pushed against him, her hips grinding gently against his crotch, where his waking manhood rose swiftly.

"It isn't that. Of course I want you. I've got a big job to do tomorrow—"

She stopped his words by pulling his face down so she could kiss his lips. Her tongue washed his lips and he opened them. For a moment there was clash of tongues and then she let his dart into her mouth. She sighed and sagged against him.

"Oh, yes!" she said as their mouths stayed welded together.

Canyon picked her up and carried her a few steps to the bed and they both sat down. His hands caressed her warm breasts and he could feel them heating up even more. He tweaked her nipples, rolled them between thumb and finger, and she moaned in delight.

"Yes, Canyon, yes! That feels so good. Makes me feel hot and wanting you. God, Canyon, yes, yes!"

He bent and kissed her breasts, moving from one to the other, then biting her nipple and at last sucking one orb into his mouth. Her hips pounded upward.

"Oh, God, Canyon! You make me so hot. Oh, damn! Uhuh, uhuh, uhuh. Oh, Christ, I'm coming." Her hips pounded again and then she fell backward on the bed, pulling him on top of her. Her whole body quivered and then shook as if a train were going past. She vibrated and her hips pounded upward at him in a rhythm. Her breath came in sobbing gasps and the long series of spasms shook her like the last leaf on an autumn tree.

At last her eyes came open and she stared at him in surprise. "Ain't nobody ever done that to me before his pecker was inside me. Damn but you are good. What's it gonna be like when you fuck me!"

She sat up and opened his pants, then pulled down his underwear and gasped at his throbbing lance.

"What a pretty boy. Christ, he'll never fit . . ." She bent and kissed the purple head of him, then moved down and pulled off his boots and socks, then jerked down his pants and underwear until he was naked.

Tears welled up in her eyes. "So beautiful! A man's body is so damn wonderful, so many hard muscles and strong chest and flat little belly, and then . . . then the good part." She bent and kissed his manhood again, then pushed Canyon down on the bed and lay beside him.

"Canyon, do anything you want. Anything. Put it in me anywhere. I want you to!"

He growled deep in his throat and pulled at her skirt. She took it down and two petticoats, then kicked off a pair of silk bloomers and stood in front of him.

Lea Jackson was a Rubens woman, all curves and soft flesh in abundance. She had surprisingly tapered legs that ended in a large bush of dark hair.

She knelt on the bed and walked across it on her knees to him. She bent so one breast came toward his mouth. Canyon touched his lips to its hot red point, sucked at it gently, then moved his tongue around it in a warm wet circle, touching the rough edges of her nipple.

Lea cried out in pure pleasure and her hands reached down for him. "Oh, yes, oh, God . . . soooooooo fine." Her voice came low and husky, lathered with desire.

Again he sucked her white mound deep into his mouth and she moaned in wonder. His hands moved down her alabaster body. Her hand caught his as it pressed hard at her round little belly, then diving into the black thatch that covered her pubic mound.

His hands caressed her, rubbed her gently all

around, and Lea's little cries came as a melody of love that spun around both of them.

He skirted the dampness of her very center and his hand moved lower with feather touches of his fingers along her soft, velvet, sensitive inner thighs. Lea cried out in wonder and joy letting the anticipation grow and build.

Her voice was like a soft purr. "Canyon, yes! God, oh, God, yes touch me there again."

His fingers traced the alabaster thighs again, causing her to writhe and jump when he touched nerve endings that were waiting for him.

"Damn, Canyon, so wonderful, so sexy . . . oh, God." Her words came in gushes from open lips twisted into a devil's smile of passion. Her thighs spread, inviting him, then closed; she rolled more on her back now and her knees lifted and again her thighs opened to him stretching upward, every part of her offering herself to him. Making her most precious part open, wanting, urging him to take her.

His fingers crept up one satin thigh, teasing, caressing, then brushing against her swollen, dripping nether lips. Lea squealed in the agony/pleasure of his touch. Her eyes opened halfway and she watched him. "Now, Canyon, dammit, fuck me now!"

He moved between her thighs and at once he felt her legs lift over his back and grip him tightly, then relax. He saw her hips hump upward, pushing her treasure spot toward him. He lowered his throbbing manhood against the softness of her well-lubricated and swollen lips.

"Please, Canyon, do me now, right now, this minute, or I'll scream and die!"

Canyon edged his shaft up to her scabbard and probed gently.

Lea squealed in ecstasy and surged upward, trapping two inches of him. Canyon moaned in satisfaction and eased forward; he bent and sucked one full breast into his mouth.

Lea screamed in wonder and thrust upward hard again and again with her hips to capture more of him. Her arms circled his hips and pulled him down on her sharply. "Marvelous! Oh, yes, wonderful. More, more! Deeper! Yes, love, push it all the way. More, more!"

Lea gasped and her eyes went wide as he thrust in until their bodies met with a crash and Lea wailed a cry of joy and rapture that lifted her to the top of the mountains. Her moaning and crooning urged him on, and her hips pounded at him in a round, grinding motion that told him that she was pleased. For the moment the flesh was all-powerful and could overcome anything and defeat anything, just so their bodies were locked together in the mating dance that was as old as man himself.

"Oh, Canyon!" She breathed it in a response to his first gentle thrustings, then he stroked a half-dozen times, sucked more on her breast, and then planted kisses around her face as she writhed against him.

Lea worked with his motions, countering them for deeper penetration, hips thrusting, twisting, writhing, making every effort to hold him, to create the friction that would excite him and herself as well.

As they worked in the dance of love, her voice took on a singsong pattern, husky, wrapped in desire and delight. Then gradually her body began to tighten against him, to grip him continually with her interior muscles, and then her body shivered and contracted and reached out until the magic trigger tripped and she powered against him with a long series of slashing, pounding climaxes that shook her like a rag doll and changed her moaning to screams of delight as she spasmed a dozen times.

At last she pushed his rump high in the air off the bed and held him there for one desperate, last bit for total pleasure, then she relaxed and fell back to the bed with him on top of her and she sighed and smiled.

Canyon had been so intent on her satisfaction that he only half-realized that in the middle of it he had climaxed himself, blasting into her with her joy and delight. He gasped for enough air to satisfy his screaming lungs. They both panted and gazed at each other in surprise and wonder.

Slowly their passion ebbed and they lay there resting. Lea's arms had come around him and he couldn't move.

She smiled at him. "Wonderful," she said softly. "Never has it been so good, so shattering, so demanding and devastating."

"Let's hope you don't write this into your story about the president," Canyon said, half-serious.

"Of course not, but it will be a fond memory forever." She let go of him and they edged apart and lay watching each other.

"Why are all the soldiers around the train? Who would try to hurt our president?"

"They are needed," he said. "Sometimes there aren't enough. Every president has a few enemies. It's just the nature of the job, the president tells me."

"You . . . you've talked with President Buchanan?" she asked, her eyes wide with wonder.

"Part of my job." He looked at the wide silver bracelet around her right wrist. He touched it. "Pretty," he said.

"My mother gave it to me as she was dying. She made me promise never to take it off. It was my mother's grandmother's special lucky bracelet. I've never let them down.''

He sat up and she came beside him, snuggling against his chest.

''You're not going to throw me out, are you?'' She reached up and kissed his lips. ''I'll even promise to let you sleep a little, after the third time.'' She giggled like a schoolgirl.

''Three would be plenty,'' Canyon said. She was much more than he had anticipated. Some women were simply better in bed than others. For just one sexy moment he wondered how Wendy Franklin would be, but dismissed it at once. Not with someone he worked with and might have to work with again. It just wasn't the smart thing to do.

She slid off the bed. ''Did you know I have some wine and cheese and apples in my reticule? A girl has to be prepared for a tough interview.''

''I still can't believe that you're a reporter.''

''I am. I'll show you my official letter the editor gave me just to convince people like you.''

''There aren't many women journalists.''

''So, somebody has to be first. I'm good at it. I get the story and can write. What difference if I'm a man or a woman?''

''It gives you an advantage. I certainly wouldn't be talking this way to a man reporter.''

They both laughed.

''I'd be tremendously disappointed if you did. Now, let's try that wine. I hope it's a good one.''

Two hours later the bottle of wine was empty, the cheese was reduced to crumbs and the apples to cores. They lay in each other's arms trying to get their wildly racing hearts and their steam-engine lungs back to normal.

"You get better and better," she said, kissing his cheek.

"Lea, where did you learn to love so deliciously?"

"Nobody teaches us, it's instinct. We just know. Like the sparrow who knows how to build a nest without learning."

"You may be right."

"Remember your very first time? You didn't have an instruction book, no teacher. It's natural and normal, and then with a little practice the refinements come."

They lay there a moment more. "I suppose you'll be riding off on your train tomorrow and I'll be trying to keep up on the regular trains."

"I imagine."

"There must be room on that last car. Couldn't you smuggle me on board?"

"Afraid not. Ten journalists from Washington wanted to come along. We had to tell them they couldn't. Too dangerous for you."

"Oh, pooh."

"Sorry, that's the rule."

"Then I better get to sleep. I have to catch the six A.M. train heading for Chicago. Otherwise I'll never catch up."

"Sorry you can't ride along. It's just not possible."

"Just think, I could keep your sleeper berth warm all afternoon."

"We don't have any berths, just a passenger car."

"Oh, well, in that case, I'll wait until you get to Chicago. What hotel will you be staying at?"

He told her before he thought about it. What the hell.

They kissed once more and went to sleep.

She was gone when he awoke in the morning, and he didn't know when she left. He quickly checked his purse and found it and his weapons intact. He had been lucky. She could have taken everything he owned and then he would never see her again.

Now he might. He dressed, shaved, and had a quick breakfast. Wendy was in the dining room and he sat with her. She smiled, looked at him with a small frown, then she smiled with deliberate effort.

"Sleep well?" she asked.

Canyon nodded. "Ready for another tough day. Maybe you'd like to take the general's place today and introduce the president."

Wendy laughed and shook her head. "Not me. That's your job. Besides, I'd never get the people quieted down. I can't yell as loud as you can."

For a moment Canyon thought she knew he had been in bed with a woman last night, but that was crazy. She couldn't know. He forgot that and turned his thoughts to the problems at hand. He had plenty. One more day of protecting the President of the United States so nobody blew his head off.

He wondered where the Blue Goose Lodge people were? Were they in town? Had they moved out on an earlier train today or yesterday? Unfortunately he would probably find out down the tracks. He had to do everything he could to be ready for them.

Breakfast was done. He let her pay her own check on the way out, then nodded.

"Come on, Franklin, we have a lot of work to do."

She watched him a moment, then walked beside him toward the nearby train depot and President Buchanan.

7

Canyon and Wendy went from the restaurant to the stationmaster's office. He looked like he hadn't slept all night. He had a bristle beard, his eyes were red and swollen, and he held two telegrams in his hand.

"Got the go ahead about two A.M." he said. "Since then we've been working on Three-eight-five, the engine I said we could use. It's ready to go now, with enough wood in the tender to take it at least four water stops. She'll stay ahead of you by half a mile."

"Good," Canyon said. "You know the engineer?"

"Best man I got. He's my brother-in-law. He'll sweep them tracks clear for you."

They thanked the stationmaster and went onto the train on the siding.

The president's car contained a bedroom and a small kitchen as well as a sitting room and his small office area. Only the president remained on the train last night. A cook had fixed him breakfast and he and General Wheeler were talking quietly when Canyon and Wendy arrived.

They were given cups of steaming black coffee and asked to sit down.

Canyon told them about the sweeper engine they would have the rest of the way into Chicago.

"Good," General Wheeler said.

"I'm glad," Canyon confessed. "I sent the wire to Chicago in your name."

The special train's engine was fired up and had taken on water and additional wood for the firebox. They left on time at the stroke of 8:30 A.M.

The first stop was Dodge Center an hour and a half out of the station. General Wheeler had not taken any more of the laudanum and said his arm was fit for duty. He carried it tenderly by his side and got ready to introduce the president.

Canyon and Wendy got off the train first, met the four men from the sheriff's office, and saw that it would be a gathering of no more than a hundred people. The four deputy sheriffs worked the crowd. One of them rode a fancy black stallion.

General Wheeler introduced the president and he started his speech. Partway through the president's talk, Canyon noticed a disturbance near the back of the crowd. He worked that way, signaled the deputy on the horse, and they moved through the crowd to where voices had been raised.

"Drop your weapon now, sir, or I'll be forced to fire."

Canyon heard the voice clearly now, Wendy's. He pushed two farmers aside and rushed forward, his own six-gun out and ready.

People faded back from the two principals. Wendy stood, legs apart, both hands on her .41-caliber weapon. The man stood twenty feet from her, a revolver in his hand, but the weapon pointed at the ground.

Canyon's first instinct was to wade in and knock down the man with the gun, but he waited on the edge of the opening.

"Put it down and you won't be charged with anything," Wendy said. The man stared at her. Wendy spoke again, her voice clear and hard. "You're violating a lawful order by your county sheriff and you could be endangering the life of the President of the United States."

"Hell, woman, I'm not hurting anybody." He started to turn, and when he was halfway around, he spun back and fired at Wendy. She fired almost at the same time she saw his weapon come up. His round missed. Hers didn't, hitting the gunman in the right shoulder, jolting the six-gun out of his hand.

He bellowed in pain and sprinted through the fringes of the crowd. Canyon raced after him. By the time Canyon got to the street, the man had mounted a bay and galloped off. O'Grady bellowed for the sheriff's deputy on the horse who had paused at the side of the affair as well. He'd had trouble getting his horse through the crowd. He came up to Canyon.

"What happened?"

"Give me your horse. I'm going after that man."

The deputy dropped off his mount. Canyon stepped into the saddle, worked through a dozen people, then hit the street and galloped after the gunman. He could still see him two blocks ahead down the town's main street. It took him another block before he saw the gunman turn to the left and angle out of town toward a river.

A half-mile out along the river, Canyon had closed the gap to fifty yards and the gunman kept looking back over his shoulder.

Canyon wanted this one alive. He rode hard, put a round over the man's head, and bellowed at him to stop.

"Pull up. Don't get yourself into more trouble." The man shook his head and kept riding. Evidently he had no other gun. Canyon fired once more in front of the horse and the man looked back, then lay down along the horse's neck and kicked his mount in the flanks with both heels.

It took another quarter-mile before Canyon overtook the big strong mount and caught the reins. He pulled the animal to a stop and scowled at the rider.

"You trying to commit suicide?" Canyon asked.

"Don't matter none," the man said.

Canyon turned the mount and led it back toward town. Then he stopped and used the man's kerchief to tie up his wounded shoulder.

"Hold that pad on your wound and maybe you won't bleed to death before I get you back to the jail."

Ten minutes later Canyon had the man in jail and ran to catch the train just as it pulled out of the station.

Wendy was there waiting for him. "What did he say?" she asked. "Why did he wave his gun around?"

"The deputy sheriff said the man was down on his luck. His wife died and his house burned down, then he lost his job. I really think he was trying to get somebody to kill him."

"My God!"

"True. But you hit his shoulder instead. Is that where you aimed?"

Tears formed in her eyes and spilled over. She shook her head. "No. It happened so fast I aimed at his chest and he moved enough so the round hit his shoulder."

"You were lucky. He the first man you've ever shot at?"

She nodded, then the tears came and Canyon helped her sit down in one of the coach seats. He put his arm around her. Her head went on his shoulder and she cried it out.

It was five minutes later when they went back to the general's small office in the end of the car for the evaluation.

"Not a threat, but a problem," Canyon said, describing the incident. "Nothing to do with the president."

"The sides on the podium are in place and should serve as a protection," General Wheeler said. "My arm is feeling better and I threw away the rest of the laudanum."

Galbreath grinned. "That's no way to turn into an opium addict. The president seemed pleased by the first stop today. He said the people were closer to him."

"Won't happen again," Lieutenant Ramstad said. "We had trouble trying to push them back after the train stopped."

The next stop was scheduled for sixty miles down the tracks. They had almost two hours.

Canyon had just leaned back against the window frame on his seat and stretched his feet out on the far side when he heard a shot from outside.

The train was going through a small cut that had been blasted out of solid rock to get down to grade level. Canyon ducked below the window and lifted up to look out. A projectile trailing three feet of cloth tail fell from above and hit a rock. The device exploded sounding like a shotgun.

At once half a dozen pellets slammed into the side of the train and cracked the window Canyon looked out.

"Everyone down below the windows," Canyon bellowed at the others in the cars. "Shotguns with double-aught buck, they're deadly."

They weren't shotguns, only the shells. Canyon had seen them used before in big towns with cobblestone streets. The outlaws used regular shotgun shells, taped ball bearings on the detonator cap in the center of the shell, and attached streamers so the shells would fall and hit on the ball bearing. They threw them off high buildings.

The same thing worked throwing them from a cliff down into a railroad cut made in solid rock. The ball bearing hit the primer charge and set off the shotgun shell, splattering double-aught buck against the train.

Canyon counted at least thirty of the rounds going off and peppering the train. He saw one window behind him blown out by a second hit by the heavy lead slugs, but no one was hurt. There was no time for the troopers to get their windows lifted and fire. Even if there had been, the attackers were fifty feet above on the edge of the cut and couldn't even be seen by those in the train.

A minute later they were through the cut and away from the danger. Canyon walked the train taking a count. One soldier had been cut by flying glass, but he was still fit for duty. The president had been taking a nap and the sounds wakened him, but when he was reassured, he went back to sleep.

General Wheeler sat down across from Canyon after both had completed their rounds.

"What a strange way to attack a train," the general said.

"Harassing attack, General. They must have known it wouldn't do much damage."

"It did get our attention."

"If that's all we have to worry about, we'll be lucky. Oh, I talked to the engineer at the last stop. He likes the idea of the engine sweeping the tracks ahead of us. He and the other engineer know each other, they will keep in sight of each other now except on sharp turns and steep hills, which we have few of. That solves one of our big worries about a track problem."

The general showed Canyon a telegram from the sheriff at the next town where they would stop.

President's train: We have picked up four men here who were talking against the president and threatening him. We are searching for three more. Suggest you bypass our town and not stop here.

Sheriff W. Bilcote.

"And the president said that we'll stop anyway," Canyon predicted.

The general nodded. "We do what we can and hope the old boy survives."

It was a moderate-sized crowd at the next stop at Leonardwood, or something like that. The little towns were all starting to look alike to Canyon, and their names now sounded alike.

The sheriff met them at the train. "Sorry, General, like I told you in the wire, it's too dangerous here. I can't allow the president to give his talk here in Leonardwood."

Canyon slipped the tail of his jacket back away from his six-gun and let his hand hang loose around the butt plate.

"Sheriff, nobody asked your opinion," Canyon said. "You were given some instructions, and some orders. Now, unless you want me to draw on you and arrest you for interfering with the President of the United States, you'll cooperate with us and put your deputies on crowd-control duties. Sheriff, do you have any questions?"

The lawman turned his hat in his hands, his eyes a little wide as he watched Canyon's hand. Sweat popped out on his forehead.

"No, sir, no questions. But I just hope to God that President Buchanan isn't shot down in my county."

There was no sign of trouble as the president went through his now-well-rehearsed talk. He left the crowd cheering.

Canyon had been at the edge of the crowd, and when he came back past the station, he saw Ambrose Galbreath talking to the telegraph clerk.

He thought nothing of it, hurried to the train, and made preparations for the departure.

They were halfway to the next town, some small place on the Chicago side of Toledo, when Canyon asked the general if he'd had Galbreath send a telegram at the last stop.

"Not me. I don't give Ambrose orders. He must have been sending a message for the president."

At the quick briefing, General Wheeler said the president had authorized them to skip two stops, since they were behind schedule. There was a reception tonight in Chicago and Buchanan was determined to be at it.

They went through the stop at the next small town, routine once more, and Canyon saw Wendy hauling a woman off toward the sheriff. He drifted along to watch. There had been no problems here except a slightly excited crowd. They had been waiting three hours for the president to arrive. Many of these folks had United States flags they were waving.

Wendy marched a woman up to the sheriff and pointed at her. "Sheriff, I've seen this woman twice before today at stops back down the line. I think she's following the president. She said you knew her."

The sheriff, a small, thin man with nervous hands and a pencil mustache, smoothed down the face hair and grinned.

"Well, Mabel. I see you got yourself in trouble again. Yep, miss, I know this woman. She works the trains, but usually at night, and almost always on a sleeper car. She's Ohio's best-known pullman car whore. Does right well financially, as I understand."

Wendy blushed. "Then she's no danger to the president?"

"Not unless she slips into his bedroom before your train leaves. In that case, the old boy might have a heart attack from overexertion."

"She won't, because I'm asking you to keep her locked up until we leave. Won't be more than ten minutes more. Or, Sheriff, you might prefer to take personal charge of her."

Wendy turned and marched away, her head held high, eyes straight ahead. She had never been so embarrassed in her life. By the time she got to the other side of the crowd, she was smiling, then a giggle slipped out. She could just imagine President Buchanan entertaining the lady in his railway bedroom.

Wendy worked the crowd, saw one man with what could have been a rifle, but it was only a hoe he had brought with him when he had seen the crowd gathering.

The president said good-bye to the people and walked into the train, and Wendy headed for the observation car. She waited until the soldiers had all filed in, then went inside and looked for Canyon. If he said anything about her picking up that whore, she would slap his face.

8

Another two hours, another stop at another small town, another rendering of the president's speech. They went through the drill again with no trouble and no problems. By this time their train had come into the state of Indiana, the very top of it, slanting over to Chicago almost due west.

As they boarded the train after the speech and good-byes, Canyon went up the steel steps behind Wendy and noticed the smooth motion of her hips under the skirt. Nice.

When they sat down in the rail car and it began to move, he looked over at her. "You still have that deck of cards?"

Wendy looked up, nodded, then grinned. "You want to play some cards?"

"Yes." He moved over to her seat and she found the cards in her small cloth traveling bag and shuffled them.

"Whist or poker?"

"Poker. It tells me more about a person's thought process and character than whist."

"Nickel a bet, dime limit."

Canyon raised an eyebrow. "You have that much money?"

"Table stakes, three-dollar maximum," she said.

"You've played poker before."

"Now and then." She shuffled and dealt. "Five-card stud, dime ante."

He searched his pockets. "I don't have any change."

"Excuses," she said, flashing soft brown eyes at him. She reached in her bag again and came up with a box of kitchen matches, blue-tipped with sulfur. She counted them out in piles of twenty.

Canyon put two one-dollar gold pieces on the bench between them and she gave him forty matches. She took forty for herself and put the rest of the matches away in her kit.

"Where did you learn to play poker?" he asked.

"I have three older brothers. They figured that poker was a good way to get my allowance each week. They beat me for four straight weeks, then I learned the game, talked to my father, and practiced with him. For the next six weeks I cleaned them out every Friday night. After that we just played for fun."

"So I walked right into your trap?"

"Maybe. Depends how good a poker player you are."

An hour later she had all of his matches but four.

General Wheeler came down the aisle. "Sorry to spoil your game, but the president just decided that we won't be stopping anymore until we get to Chicago. If we highball right through, we can still make it in time for his reception. We'll stop a minute at the next station and wire ahead for clearance the rest of the way to Chicago. Hope I don't ruin the rest of your day."

"Not at all," Canyon said. "I'll tell Lieutenant Ramstad." He hesitated. "What will our duties be in the big city?"

"Next to nothing. The Chicago Police Department will take over security for the president. They pick him up at the station and will bring him back two days later just in time to head back on the train to Washington.''

"You're giving us a two-day vacation in the big town?''

"About the size of it. I'm going to see a good doctor the first day. You guys can see the sights. Just don't get in any trouble.''

He waved and went back to the front of the car. The soldiers sent up a shout of joy when Canyon told them about rolling straight through to Chicago.

Wendy waited for him to come back from his walk.

Canyon sat down and looked at his four matches. "Showdown for the rest of my stake," he said. Canyon won. He played seven-card showdown for the eight matches and he won again. Once more he played seven-card showdown for the sixteen and won.

"Now, let's play some hard-nosed poker," Canyon said. He played carefully, watching her reactions. It took almost another hour for him to wipe out her stack of matches. He picked up the four one-dollar gold pieces from the bank and pocketed them, then pushed the matches over to her.

"You're good," Wendy said. "Did you just let me win those first few hands?''

"You'll never know. Where did you grow up with these three brothers?''

"Washington. My father was in government service." She looked up and he liked the way her nose tipped up just a little. "Where did you grow up? Are you from Ireland?''

"It's a long story," Canyon said.

"We have another five or six hours until we get to Chicago.''

He shrugged. "It's a boring story, but I can stand it if you can.''

"I'll risk it. I paid two dollars to hear it.''

Canyon chuckled. "My mother and father were both born in Ireland."

"But how did you get such an interesting name as Canyon?"

"My mother picked it out. She was always reading books and looking at paintings and drawings about America. I was almost due to be born when my father told my mother we were fleeing from Ireland and heading for America.

"Mother wanted to pick out a name that would fit the spirit of America, so she came up with Canyon. I was born shortly thereafter in Ireland, and at my baptism our parish priest would have nothing of a name like Canyon. Quickly I was named Michael Patrick O'Grady, but my parents never called me anything but Canyon."

"Right after you were born, you all had to come to America," Wendy said. "Was that due to the great potato famine?"

"Partly, but mostly because of the British police. Father was one of the founders of the Young Ireland Movement. That made him a close friend of the other founders Fintan Lalor and Padraic Pearse, names the British constabulary knew well.

"Such association was more than enough to have the British searching for Father. When we fled, the British had a price on Father's head. So we came to America, a young family with a baby boy named with a nod to yesterday and a hope for tomorrow."

"Canyon O'Grady," Wendy said softly. "It does have a certain lilt to it."

"As a small child it did cause me a few fights. My father went to work in the gangs that built the railroads in the East. As I grew up, I knew construction work would not be for me. I wanted something with a lot more danger and adventure. That was when I went west to the American frontier."

Wendy watched him, her pretty face now serious. "Did you ever go back to Ireland?"

"Father went back twice. he took me with him both times as a cover so the police wouldn't suspect him. We stayed there for two years each time. I was in Ireland when I was six to eight years old and then again from twelve to fourteen."

"So your father continued to work in the Irish revolutionary movement."

"He probably did. He put me in the hands of a group of learned friars who pounded everything they knew into their wee visitor from America. Any education I have that shows is their fault."

"More likely to their credit, Canyon O'Grady." She looked at him, an open smile that hid nothing, and he could see the interest, the curiosity, the wondering if their relationship would progress past official business.

"Later I had learned a lot about the West, how to live in it, about the people. I lived one summer with an Indian friend who taught me the Indian ways, worked some wagon trains and some trail drives of cattle, and then went back to Washington and looked for a job."

"No wonder they hired you as a special agent. You have perfect qualifications. Now I wonder how I ever got in."

They were quiet for a moment and Canyon realized with a start that there was no great need to talk. He felt comfortable with this woman. Good, that would make working with her the next four days that much easier.

"What . . . what are you going to do in Chicago?" Wendy asked.

"I've been there before. There are some interesting

buildings to see, some places to go. The lake looks like an ocean it's so huge.''

"I've never been there," she said, watching him.

"Oh. Well, I guess I could give you the guided tour.''

"That would be marvelous!'' Her brown eyes shone and she moved some of her long blond hair back from her face. She had a great smile.

"Good, done. We'll hire a rig and I'll drive you all over town. We'll have lunch at some picturesque little spot and then a fancy dinner in one of the fine restaurants.''

"I'll pay my half," she said quickly.

Canyon frowned. "No such thing. I have all of my poker earnings. I think I'll blow the whole wad on a real two-day vacation.''

"Sounds like fun.''

"It will be." He stood. "Right now I'm going to relax. Trains always make me sleepy. I'm going to find one of those pillows that they have on board and lean back against the window and have myself a little nap. Oh, did we eat anything at noon?''

Wendy laughed. "I really don't remember. We'll try to get something at the next station we stop at. Some of these towns have small little cafés right in the stations.''

They rolled into Chicago a little after ten o'clock that night and the president was hurried directly to the reception that had been waiting for him for two hours. He would go from there to the Grand Hotel. Chicago police took over security as soon as the president stepped off the train.

The rest of the staff went by carriage to the Grand. They were a floor below the president. The soldiers were quartered at the Chicago Armory.

Canyon and Wendy checked in and went to their

assigned rooms. They were just down the hall from each other. By that time it was nearly midnight.

Wendy hesitated at her door. ''Canyon,'' she said. He turned toward her and she reached up and kissed him. He was surprised. Automatically his arms came around her and he pulled her close.

She broke the kiss and leaned back a little to see him better. ''I'm hoping that's a smile,'' she said.

''It's a big smile.''

Canyon returned the kiss and it was soft and sweet. They broke it when another couple walked toward them down the hall.

Wendy bent and unlocked her door and opened it a little. She looked at Canyon and stepped inside but blocked the way. ''Let me try that once more,'' she said.

They kissed, softly, gently, their bodies barely touching. She pulled away and edged the door in front of her.

''Now I'll have something to dream about tonight,'' Wendy said. She smiled at him and closed the door.

Canyon nodded and went down the hall to his room. They had agreed to meet at her room at eight-thirty for breakfast, then to start their grand tour. He thought about Wendy and the kisses only for a moment. She was a fine lady and wasn't about to jump into bed with him. Fine. She was fun to be with and he'd have no trouble working with her the rest of the mission.

He undressed and dropped on the bed and slept almost at once.

The tour went even better than Canyon had hoped. He had been in Chicago only once before. They hired a rig for Canyon to drive and wandered around, stopped for lunch at a small little café that sold only Italian food, and drove along Lake Shore Drive.

"The lake does look like an ocean," Wendy said. "Are you sure they aren't fooling us and this is really the Pacific Ocean?"

Canyon laughed. He hadn't felt so relaxed in months. Now that he thought of it, he hadn't had any vacation days for a long time. He enjoyed this to the fullest, knowing that it would be back to work the day after tomorrow.

He pulled up to a vacant lot on the lakefront and tied the reins.

He looked at Wendy, who wore a frilly yellow dress today, much more feminine than her working clothes. She looked like a blooming daffodil. Canyon turned to her and smiled. "Figured it was time I did a little research."

"Oh, what kind of research?" Her brown eyes were serious, her face ready to smile but holding back.

"I wondered if your kisses are as sweet during the daylight as they were at night."

Now the smile broke out and she laughed softly, her pale-brown eyes dancing now. "Only one way to find out, Canyon O'Grady."

She met him for the kiss. This time it was harder, more demanding, and when it ended, she pulled back, her eyes wide, and she gave a little sigh.

"Oh, my," Wendy said.

Canyon frowned. "No, I can't tell yet."

"Then you better—"

His lips cut off her words and he kissed her again. This time he pulled her toward him until her breasts pressed hard against his chest. It was a long kiss and she moved firmly against him, her arms around him holding him tightly.

The kiss ended and their lips parted only an inch.

"Yes, I like that, Canyon."

"Now I know," he said. "Your kisses are even better during the daylight hours. Of course, there'll have to be more testing and research." He pecked a kiss on her nose.

"There's a big building up north a ways I haven't ever known what it is. I wondered last time I was here. I figure we should go take a look. By then it should be almost time for a long delicious dinner somewhere. Maybe we can find a place that looks out over the lake and we could watch the sun set on the water."

"Does it do that?"

"We'll find out."

About four o'clock they turned in the rig and walked to a fancy restaurant they had seen. It wasn't over the water. Wendy had frog legs because she had never eaten them before. Canyon played it safe with a big thick steak.

They walked back to the hotel, about six blocks away. At her door, Wendy didn't hesitate. She unlocked it, opened the door wide, and looked for a match beside the lamp on the dresser. When the kerosene lamp glowed brightly, she turned down the wick and motioned to Canyon.

"Don't stand out there in the hall. Someone might see you."

He stepped in and Wendy closed the door. She took off the small hat she had worn and put it beside the lamp.

"Now, Canyon O'Grady, one more experiment about kisses after dark."

Canyon hesitated. "You really think that we should carry out that experiment? What if it's a success?"

Wendy smiled softly and cocked her head to one side. "Well, that's a chance I'll just have to take, isn't it?"

She touched his shoulders and then they came together slowly; his lips found hers and the gentleness was there again, a light, feathery kiss that stirred Canyon more than he wanted to admit. He let the kiss linger a moment, then eased away.

"I really shouldn't be here," Canyon said.

"I know." She kept her arms around him and reached up to be kissed again.

This time there was more wanting, more emotion, and she sighed as they kissed, her lips tightly together. He wondered if she waited for his tongue to brush them apart. The two eased away from each other and she caught his hand and pulled him to the bed, where they both sat down.

Wendy looked at him in the soft light of the lamp. "Canyon O'Grady, what's happening? Can you tell me?"

"A beautiful girl is getting kissed and both of the people like the feeling. That's what's happening."

"Again."

He bent to find her lips and this time they were parted. He opened his as well and his tongue explored into her mouth, then retreated. Her tongue moved into him a moment, then drifted back. He could hear her breathing surge faster and faster. She came away from his lips and leaned heavily against him, her breasts crushing against his chest.

"So sweet and soft and gentle. So wonderful. You completely undo me, Canyon O'Grady." She eased away and found his hand and pushed it down the front of her dress.

"Wendy—"

She shushed him with a quick kiss. "It's all right. I want you to touch me. No man has ever touched my breasts before."

His hand found her breast, warm and soft. He held it a moment, then his fingers explored and touched her nipple and she gasped. He rubbed it between his thumb and finger and sensed that it was surging and growing.

"Please kiss me, Canyon."

He moved his hand a little so he could reach in and kiss her quivering lips. He saw a tear slip down her cheeks and gently he took his hand away from her breast.

The kiss was full and sweet but somehow different now. She ended it and looked up at him, tears seeping from both eyes now.

"Please hold me tight, Canyon O'Grady. Please."

He held her and she snuggled against him more like a small child than a woman, and he knew that she had passed through a portal, a new experience, and now she needed some time to absorb it, to evaluate it and adjust to the new feelings that were assaulting her.

"Did you like my touching you?" he asked.

"Oh, yes! But I'm afraid I liked it too much. I . . . I wanted you to touch me all the time, to . . . to touch me lower."

"But you decided now wasn't the time?"

"Yes, I decided." She pushed back and looked up at him. "Oh, not because you were with me. If anyone does . . . I mean, when some man does . . . I mean . . . I guess I wish that it might be you, Canyon O'Grady. But not tonight."

"There's no hurry. Remember the first time happens only once. It can never be taken back or happen again. Take your time."

He held her for another ten minutes before she shivered, then eased away from him and kissed him lightly on the lips.

"Mr. O'Grady, I think you better go now. I don't feel at all brazen right now. I still feel all warm and wonderful and I want to think about that for a while. Would that be all right?"

He kissed her nose and lifted away from the bed. "That would be fine, Miss Franklin. You never did tell me something. Are you related to Benjamin Franklin?"

Wendy laughed and he knew it was going to be all right with her.

"No, not that we can tell. I'm not even sure if he had any children. My mother tried to trace his family tree once, but that got everyone confused."

Five minutes later, Canyon lay on his bed down the hall and thought a moment about the lovely girl he'd been working with for the past three days. She was a special lady. Then he went to sleep and dreamed of wading down a river of blood to stop a canoe filled with black powder that was going to ram the president's train when it went through a ford on a creek. He knew trains never forded creeks, but he didn't have time to tell that to the three blue geese that were paddling the canoe.

9

General Wheeler caught both Canyon and Wendy as they came down to breakfast the next morning. He motioned them to one side.

"We're going to be working today, after all. There's been an impromptu parade scheduled for today just after noon. I want the two of you to check out the route, report any hazards, and give your approval before ten o'clock. There's a carriage waiting outside for your tour. Anything that looks dangerous at all, tell the rig full of Chicago policemen behind you and they'll try to solve the problem. We're talking about gun shops, old cannons aimed at the street, anything you think is a problem."

"At least we had a tour of the city yesterday," Wendy said. "How is your arm feeling, General Wheeler?"

He lifted his left arm almost to his shoulder, winced, and put it down. "Could be better. I'm not going to sign up for any bare-knuckled boxing matches just yet."

"We have time for breakfast before we leave?" Canyon asked.

General Wheeler nodded. "A fast breakfast."

The inspection trip turned out to be mostly a waste of time. They found four drunks sleeping on the sidewalk and had the police move them into a deep alley.

Already there were barricades up to stop normal wagon and buggy traffic on the parade route.

People were starting to gather as they retraced the route. Word spread fast in the big city.

When they first sat in the carriage, Wendy looked at Canyon with a touch of shyness.

"Canyon, about last night—"

"Wendy, last night was delightful. I'll remember it for a long time. I have no regrets, do you?"

"No, of course not. I just didn't want you to think—"

"I think that you're a lovely young woman, delightful, loving, tender, intelligent. A lady who knows what she wants and isn't in a rush to charge into anything." He paused and watched her smile. "Oh, and anytime you want to do more research into that kissing subject, I'm more than ready to help."

"Now you are teasing me," she said, her smile wider.

"Not at all. Let's check out this parade route."

The parade went off as scheduled. The Chicago officials had set it two weeks in advance, they just hadn't bothered to tell the president or his party about it.

The parade and its reception afterward took up the rest of the day. Just after supper the general and his staff had a meeting in the general's room.

The usual evaluation group was there.

"We have an early-morning departure, so I'd suggest you limit your night activities. We'll leave the station at six A.M. The president wants to get back to his scheduled stops. He has nine tomorrow. We should get to somewhere in Ohio for our layover, then the president wants to do another ten stops the next day, with us arriving in Washington just after eight P.M."

"Doesn't he remember those attempts to assassinate him coming out here?" Canyon asked.

"He remembers, but we've kept them all out of the

newspapers. I'm not sure just how we did that, but so far, so good, President Buchanan says. So, we're doing it again."

"What happened to those other three Blue Goose Lodge members we ran off at that one town?" Canyon asked.

"Let's hope we don't see them again," Ambrose Galbreath said. The president's adviser on economic affairs usually only listened at the meetings. But now and then he had a good suggestion.

"Anything else?" General Wheeler asked.

"I'd like to keep the people at least twenty yards back from the observation car," Lieutenant Ramstad said. "We need to get out of the car quicker and form our line, then have the car pull another ten yards away from us."

"Sounds good," Wheeler said. "Easier than pushing a thousand people back ten yards. So, all of you have a good night's sleep and we'll see you first thing in the morning. Everyone at the station by five-thirty."

The others left the general's room and Canyon walked Wendy back to her room. She stood with her back against the door, making no move to open it.

"Research time?" Canyon asked.

Wendy smiled. "You seem to enjoy your researching, Mr. O'Grady."

"I must say I do enjoy it."

A couple passed in the hallway, glanced at them, and went on by.

Canyon leaned forward and she met him. Only their lips touched, a gentle kiss that surprised Canyon with its intensity. He pulled away slowly and her eyes were still closed. For a moment she lost her balance and he caught her.

"My goodness," Wendy said. "So . . . so nice."

"Early call in the morning," Canyon said, his voice husky.

"Yes, early." She reached out and kissed him again, then spun, opened her door, and hurried inside. The door closed and then opened enough to show her face.

"See you tomorrow, Mr. O'Grady."

"You better."

The door shut slowly and Canyon walked down to his room surprisingly cheerful. This tall, slender woman had more of an effect on him than anyone he could remember. He closed his door and dropped on the bed. Morning would come early.

Lea Jackson had seen President Buchanan twice today. Once when he left the Grand Hotel to go to the parade, and again in the parade. There had been no chance either time for her or her two men.

Now she touched her newest weapon, a double-barreled shotgun. She had sawed off the barrels. She had fired shotguns before, knew the devastation they could create. With double-aught buck she could kill everyone on the platform of that damn train.

With both barrels she could do the job. It all depended how much she wanted to do it. If she killed the president, the guards would surely execute her on the spot. Was his death that important to her?

Right now it seemed as if it were, but she would think on it. She would try a few other ideas first. As her ace in the hole she still had the railroad bridge at McClarren, Pennsylvania. This time they would be going the other direction so she would be on the town side of the bridge.

That would be her last try.

Before that, the president planned on stopping at all nine stations tomorrow and nine or ten the next day. They would leave at six A.M., so she had to take a train tonight to get ahead of them. She would take a local train out to the second stop the presidential train would make. Yes. There they would have a surprise for the guards.

This time they would do it right. She nodded and walked toward the train station. There was a train leaving at a little after eight tonight. She and her remaining two men would be on it. She had purposefully not contacted Canyon O'Grady at the hotel.

She didn't see how such a talk would help, and while she would love to make love to him again, she had more important things to plan. She lugged her heavy suitcase to the train station and bought a ticket, then got on the first coach as they had planned.

Twenty pounds of black powder seemed heavier now than it had when she bought it yesterday. She had the powder, the fuses, and the rest of her surprise. The sawed-off shotgun fit in a slightly larger carpetbag she had bought.

Lea worried until she saw both of her men get on the train. Meckley had grinned and then sat down just behind her. After this was over . . . No, she refused to think any farther ahead than the glorious death of the president. Then she could plan the rest of her life. First, James Buchanan!

The Presidential Special pulled out of Chicago promptly at six A.M. and headed east. It went through two small towns and then another. Ten more miles down the tracks the trail headed into the village of Baderville. No stop was planned there, but suddenly the train took a quick turn onto a siding.

The train's brakes slammed on, steel wheels locked against the steel rails, and sparks flew as the train ground to a slower and slower rate.

The end of the siding came up suddenly and the

engineer tried to reverse the drive wheels on the big locomotive. They were locked in place, spewing sparks all over the siding.

The passengers in the two cars in back of the engine were jolted at the sudden switch to the siding, and now everyone hung on to the seats as the train slowed down from thirty-five miles an hour.

"We can't stop her," the engineer screamed at the fireman. Both men held on as the end bunker at the last section of track came up quickly. The brakes bit in harder and steel screeched on steel, then there was a jolt as the big ram intended to stop rolling freight cars hit the front of the engine.

It drove the ram six feet back into the side of the hill and then the Presidential Special stopped.

President Buchanan was thrown off his chair in his living-room section. Three of the soldiers crashed to the floor. Wendy jolted off the seat and landed on Canyon O'Grady, who braced his feet against the seat ahead of him and held the girl tightly.

When the train settled back to a stop, everyone started talking at once.

Canyon jumped off the train and ran down to the engine. "What happened?"

The engineer shook his head. "Some damn fool switched us onto the siding. We were cleared to high-ball straight through. Wait until I get my hands on that switchman."

"Will the train still run? Can you back us out of here?"

The engineer nodded. "Don't think anything is hurt too much. Let me try."

A moment later the train began to back up toward the switch. Canyon ran ahead along the siding until he came to the offending switch. It was still set to divert the next train into the siding. He made sure it stayed that way as the train backed out onto the main line.

Canyon could see the sweeper engine stopped two hundred yards down the tracks.

He looked around the switch that had done the foul deed. Six feet behind it he found a man dressed in trainman overalls. His throat had been slit and he lay crumpled in death beside another set of tracks.

"Blue Goose Lodge," Canyon said softly. The bastards had got here, killed the switchman, then set the switch to put the train into the short siding.

Lieutenant Ramstad ran up with three men. They saw what had happened.

"Anybody hurt on the train?" Canyon asked.

"Don't think so," Ramstad said. "The president fell off his chair, but he's fine."

"Let's get this thing back on the tracks and moving forward."

Ten minutes later they were back in position, the switch was thrown, sending them east down the main line, and they got ready for the first stop of the day.

Canyon didn't even know the name of this small Illinois town. Everything went according to plan and they pulled away promptly fifteen minutes after they stopped.

General Wheeler motioned to Canyon and Wendy. "Let's talk," he said. They sat in the general's seats and all were quickly of the same mind. Canyon put it into words.

"We go back there and simply demand that the president scrap the rest of the stops and head straight through to Oakville, Ohio. We'll stay overnight there so we don't have to travel at night, and the next day we go straight to Washington with no speech stop."

General Wheeler and Wendy nodded and they went

back to the president's car. He was talking with Ambrose Galbreath.

"Mr. President, we've got something of a crisis on our hands here," General Wheeler said. "This Blue Goose Lodge is getting too active. They seem to know what we're going to do. It's our suggestion that we cancel all further stops and speeches."

"Afraid of that, Rufus," James Buchanan said. "Much as I hate to, I agree with you. Can we go straight through, then?"

"Sir, we suggest that we return to Oakville, Ohio, where we stayed overnight on the way out. That's about halfway. We stay there overnight as before. We can get there before dark. If we try to run on through the night, there are too many problems that can crop up. We couldn't see anything on the tracks and it might be put there after our sweeper engine passed."

The president looked at Ambrose. "Mr. Galbreath, what's your feeling on this matter?"

"I like the stops. The exposure does you good, but these folks are the experts in protecting you. I'd have to go along with them."

"All right, tell the engineer. I'd guess we'll still need to stop for wood and water for the engine. Lord knows I have enough work to do without making those speeches. I did enjoy talking with the people, though. I should have done this much earlier in my time in office."

"Thank you, Mr. President," Canyon said, and the three of them trooped back to their car.

"I'll write out a telegram and have the conductor drop it off at the next station. He has a little leather bag he tosses out at the stationmaster when we don't stop," Wheeler said.

Canyon rubbed his jaw. "So, we have the small-town stops ruled out as potential dangers. What else is there? The Blue Goose Lodge is still out there gunning for our president.''

"Obstruction on the tracks," Wendy said. "We could ask that sweeper engine to stay closer to the train—say, no more than a hundred yards separating them. That wouldn't give anyone time to pull a wagon or some other device on the tracks after the sweeper passed and before our train gets there.''

"We'll do it," the general said. "Just as soon as we can get in touch with the engineer up there.''

"Then there's always the bomb," Canyon said. "The kind the Blue Goose Lodge planted on the way out that we barely got across in time. They could set up another bomb on the tracks and simply light it after the sweeper goes past. That danger we have to worry about until we get the president back in the White House.''

"No way we can protect against that," General Wheeler said. "We might put a rifleman in the engine cab or on the wood tender. He could scan the tracks ahead and shoot up anyone he saw trying to plant a bomb.''

"Except it might just be a couple of small boys playing along the tracks," Wendy said. "Kids do that.''

"So, we'll be careful," Wheeler said. "Canyon, ask Lieutenant Ramstad for his best marksman. We'll place him in the tender as soon as we stop.''

Canyon nodded. He looked around. No one else could hear what they were saying.

"One more thing bothers me. Who knew when we were leaving the station this morning?''

General Wheeler shrugged. "Only the usual, the soldiers, you two, the president, and his three advisers.''

"There wasn't an announcement made to the press or even to the stationmaster?''

"No, we had the engine crew on board at four A.M. It could have been anytime after that. Why, Canyon?"

"Seems that the Blue Goose Lodge knows what we're doing and where the president is going to be every minute. They knew the stops where he'd talk and those that were missed. They knew when we left this morning. It's too coincidental. In this work I learn to mistrust coincidences."

General Wheeler squinted and looked at Canyon. "Son, you're telling me that we've got a spy on board this train?"

"I can't figure out any other explanation. We send telegrams. A spy on board could also send telegrams at every station we stop at, or by throwing a message off the train where we don't stop."

"I hate to think it," General Wheeler said. "There are so damn few people it could be."

"But that makes it easier," Wendy said.

"In a way," the general admitted.

"Now all we have to do is figure out a way to catch the spy before he becomes an assassin," Canyon said. "If the Blue Goose Lodge can't kill the president from the outside, the spy would have that as his last and final act. It would be suicide for him."

"So all we need is a way to trap the man," General Wheeler said.

"That's all," Wendy agreed. She looked at Canyon. "Let's get back to our seats and work on some ideas."

10

Canyon O'Grady paced up and down the aisle of the coach as the train rolled along toward the east. They had already passed the next place they were supposed to stop at, but they sped through without even a whistle and the crowd didn't know that they wouldn't be seeing the president.

Canyon slid into the seat beside Wendy, who had out a pad and paper and had been writing down ideas.

"Suspects," Canyon said. "The twenty soldiers are out. The lieutenant and his sergeant keep them too closely controlled for them to send any telegrams. Lieutenant Ramstad is a suspect, since one person on board the train must be the spy. You and I and the general are also suspects, but I rule the three of us out. Who does that leave?"

"The engineer, the fireman, three more train employees, and the three presidential advisers," Wendy said.

"Right. The trainmen were selected after a complete background check. Chances are it isn't any one of them. How would they know what to tell the Blue Goose Lodge people? They wouldn't."

"That narrows it down to Ramstad and the three advisers," Wendy said.

"It isn't Ramstad. I know men, and he couldn't be doing it. Which leaves the three advisers."

Wendy got up and paced the aisle this time. When she came back after the second trip, she was grinning. "Got it! We make some phony plans. We decide in a regular evaluation meeting that we do something. It will be some stop or side trip that the spy will think so important he has to notify the Blue Goose people."

Canyon nodded. "Good, good. Yes. Now, for the message. What would upset them the most? They must know we plan on staying overnight at Oakville. We could make plans like we have decided to stop fifty miles sooner. You have that map?"

Wendy took it from her traveling bag and spread it out. It showed the train route through northern Ohio.

"Garberville," Canyon said. "It's about fifty miles short of where we'll be staying. This means the Blue Goose people would have any attacks planned for our overnight at the wrong spot. Also they would see us go through and have to try to catch up and get ahead of us again."

Wendy nodded. "Yes, yes, it should work. Let's go see General Wheeler and tell him all about our idea. Then have our evaluation meeting with just the five us, including Ambrose Galbreath. He could be the one. If he isn't, he must be telling the other two advisers everything we plan."

They talked with General Wheeler. He nodded. "Only, how do we keep tabs on the three advisers? They usually spend most of their time in that back section of the president's car."

Canyon waved a hand. "No problem. The president is quite a poker player, I hear. After our evaluation meeting when we plant the phony plans, you go in and get the president and the other three into a low-stakes poker game. Then I'll arrange for us to stop at the next small station. The conductor has some method of telling the engineer to stop.

"The one who leaves the poker game at or near the station is our prime suspect."

General Wheeler laughed softly. "Canyon, I should put you in our new intelligence division we're starting for the army. You know how to be sneaky."

A half-hour later the seeds were planted. General Wheeler had a short talk alone with the president, then they got the poker game going. Ambrose Galbreath had been at the planning session and had plenty of time to tell his buddies when the train would be stopping for the night.

A little over an hour later, the train pulled up at a small town where they were not scheduled to give a speech. Canyon stood in the connector between the two cars and peered out between the leathers at the small railroad station.

General Wheeler was watching out the president's one unshielded window. Less than twenty seconds after the train stopped, a man swung down and walked quickly toward the station. It was colder outside again, and the man had on a heavy overcoat and a hat that Canyon couldn't remember seeing before. Once the man looked over his shoulder, then hurried inside the station.

Canyon ran to the near end of the building where there were no windows, and then slid around the side. At the first window he saw the man talking with the telegrapher. He pushed a piece of paper to the telegraph key man, who nodded and began tapping out a message.

A minute later he was done. The man held out his hand and took the paper back, paid for the wire, then rushed out of the station and ran for the train.

Canyon waited for a moment, then walked into the station, showed his identification, and demanded to know what the message was the man had just sent.

"I shouldn't do that, against company rules," the telegrapher said.

"I'll arrest you and charge you with a federal crime if you don't tell me now!"

The man wrote out the message on a paper and gave it to Canyon. He read it on his way to the train. General Wheeler said he'd tell the conductor to hold the train until Canyon came back.

The message said, "To Phyllis Jones, Oakville, Ohio. Staying overnight at Garberville, Ohio. Meet you there. Signed, B. Jones."

"Got him," Canyon said. He ran for the presidential car steps and swung on board. The conductor waved at the engineer and the train moved out of the station.

In the president's living-room area sat the man in the topcoat. General Wheeler was shouting at him. The man's hat was off and now Canyon could see that he was Ambrose Galbreath.

"Get it?" General Wheeler asked Canyon.

Canyon nodded and handed the piece of paper to the general. He read it and backhanded Galbreath across the face.

"Bastard," General Wheeler shouted. He dived for the man, but Ambrose hit the general in his wounded shoulder and dug into his own overcoat pocket.

Almost too late Canyon realized the man was drawing a weapon. O'Grady lunged forward, slammed his shoulder into Galbreath as he came upright. The spy's hand was out of his right-hand pocket now and held a derringer.

There was a roar as the little gun went off. President Buchanan dived out of his chair to the carpet and by then Canyon had Galbreath on the floor. He slammed his fist down on the hand that held the derringer and it skittered from numb fingers.

"Bastard," General Wheeler shouted again, and kicked the adviser in the side. The tall man on the floor tried to double up his legs, then gagged twice and vomited as the kick into his kidney produced the results the general had tried for.

Canyon pocketed the little gun, saw it was a .45 with two shots, and pushed his boot into Galbreath's back, pinning him to the floor.

"I should kick him about three times in the head," General Wheeler said, fuming. "Then we wouldn't need to worry about a trial."

President Buchanan lifted off the floor and settled in his chair. He was unharmed.

"None of that, Rufus. We'll charge him with attempted murder and let the courts deal with him. I would suggest you tie him hand and foot and put a guard over him until we get to Washington."

The president looked at Canyon. "Well, young man, it looks like you've done it again. This time you've probably saved my life. He had that derringer pointed dead-center on my heart before you slammed him sideways."

"Always glad to help out when I can, Mr. President. Right now I need to go talk to the troops. There's going to be all twenty of those soldiers guarding this car all night long while we're in Oakville."

The rest of the day drifted past. They stopped at spots for wood and water where no crowds waited. They roared through Garberville and Canyon had a enjoyable moment waving through the window at the Blue Goose Lodge plotters who must be out there somewhere.

He talked with the troops, then played cards with Wendy and was ready for a good night's sleep when they parked the train on a siding in Oakville and he went up to a room in the hotel. Wendy had gone to the hotel first and he had planned on not seeing her tonight. They had one more day and then perhaps they could meet and talk and . . . even research some more.

He unlocked his door and stepped into the room. Before he closed the door, he froze against the wall, instantly aware that someone else was in the room. He drew his six-gun fast and peered into the dim light that came in from the hallway.

Then a woman laughed lightly and he started to relax.

"Don't just sit on the bed laughing," Canyon said. "Light the lamp so I don't shoot you full of holes." He cocked the six-gun so the person could hear it.

Feet scrambled across the floor, a match struck, and in the glow he saw the girl. She lit the wick on the lamp, put on the chimney, and turned down the wick so it was bright but wouldn't smoke.

"Lea," he said, surprised. She wore only a thin silk nightdress. "I didn't see you in Chicago."

"You can see me now. I was too busy in Chicago covering the president's reception and his speeches and the parade. I was on my way back to Washington, then stopped here, wondering if the president's train might stop here again. Lucky me."

"Lucky me," Canyon said. "I was figuring on nothing more interesting than a long night's sleep."

"Don't let me stop you," Lea said. She let the nightdress slip off her shoulders, and a moment later it was only a shimmering pile around her feet.

"That's not fair, Lea."

"I know. That's what makes it so much fun." She shook her head, swinging her short dark hair and making her breasts sway and bounce.

"Canyon O'Grady, I've thought about you since that time we made love here in this town. It was wonderful. Do you think we can replay that scene and make it as good as it was? I've been wanting you ever since we parted.''

"Might give it a try.''

She walked the few feet to him, her hips swinging, her breasts shaking and rolling. He caught one orb with his hand and held it.

"Oh, yes, Canyon.'' Then she was against him, her bare body pressing from ankle to breasts against him, her hips starting to rotate in that little dance. He picked her up and carried her to the bed, went back, and put the room's only chair under the door handle so anyone coming in would have to break the chair first.

She lay on the bed waiting, one leg bent slightly, her breasts rising and sinking as her breath came fast.

He bent and, without touching any of the rest of her, kissed her hot lips. They tried to devour him, and he responded. His fingers brushed lightly over her shoulders and then her neck, then down to her chest. She shuddered and cried out in delight.

His hands caressed her breasts, large orbs with pink areolae and browned, rough nipples. He rubbed them and squeezed them and slowly they rose and filled and grew before his eyes.

"Oh, God,'' she said softly.

Her hips began to rotate gently, but she couldn't reach him. He lay gently by her side and her hands caught at his clothes, pulling open buttons, lifting his shirt from his pants, pushing away his jacket.

Canyon's hands explored her breasts a moment more, cupping them in their warmth and then trailing down her flat little belly and across the rise where her thick swatch of black hair covered her.

"Oh, yes, down there, damn! Yes, yes!'' Her arms wrapped around his neck, pulled him down on top of her, and her lips found his again, her tongue darting into his mouth at once. Her heat built and built and soon Canyon knew his own blood was rising.

She pulled at his pants, then jerked down his underdrawers, and he kicked them off.

"Oh, yes, the good parts!" She caught at his growing manhood. He stirred and grew and she coaxed him, then cried out in wonder as he was firm and stood tall. She bent and kissed his head and then down his shaft.

"I love it, God help me but I love it so," Lea said, her voice husky with desire.

He pulled her up and turned on his back, lifting her over him so her breasts swung free. He caught one in his mouth and Lea cried out in joy.

"Oh, love, delicious, so good. So . . . so good!"

She caught her hands in his flame-red hair and she played with it. "Wonderful hair. Ain't never seen anything like it before."

His hands caressed her other breast and then moved slowly down her belly to the swatch of blackness; he entered the tangle. She cried out in wonder, then moved so he could lick and chew on her other breast.

His hands worked through the maze and touched the dampness, then the soft pink lips, and Lea humped downward at him.

"Oh, sweet Jesus! Oh, yes, yes, yes. I want you down there. Oh, God!" She fell to the side and turned on her back, her legs spread, and she pushed his hand back to her crotch. Canyon's fingers found the soft wetness again and she spread her legs wider, humping upward just enough to make contact with his fingers. He slipped one into her, and Lea crooned and moaned, her hips doing their dance to accept him.

Her hand caught his shaft and pulled him toward her. "God, Canyon, now, please. Oh, please now! Fill me up now and make me complete. Now, Canyon."

He slid over one bare leg and nestled between her white soft inner thighs. Her hand directed him. He hovered over her a moment and then she had him in place and her arms went around his hips and pressed him forward.

Her cries became a wild moan of desire and surrender and a moan of acceptance as he slid gently into her wet softness, throbbing and pulsating, wanting now more than anything on earth to mate with her, to drive in deeply inside the cage of flesh, to plant his seed as man had done for thousands and thousands of years.

Lea countered his every thrust, pressing forward when he did, easing off, then accepting more and more of him until he was buried inside her and her moans gave way to soft mewing and a kind of purr that told him she was satisfied for the moment.

They both remained perfectly still for thirty seconds. Both could feel the pressure mounting and mounting until neither could stand it. Then they cried out in ecstasy and he pushed forward, thrusting, and she matched his drive.

She crooned and moaned in a rhythmic crescendo of delight as they pounded faster and harder, each matching the other. Their heat built until it was beyond them, their bodies were obeying only their own rules and directives, the human species was perpetuating itself in the dance of love.

Suddenly Lea let out one hoarse, throaty yell. Her eyes went wide, her mouth came open to scream. Only a guttural moan emerged and her whole body writhed and shook as her cries went up an octave and her torso spasmed and shook. Lea let it all build until she exploded with a scream of raw passion satisfied. She rocked and bounced another half-minute before she gasped and sucked in air and then fell to the mattress, spent and drained and totally satisfied.

Canyon had kept something in reserve, and when she was finished, he thrust harder and harder, lifting his knees higher and punching into her with a fury that he had seldom known. The world was growing smaller and smaller as the pressure built until somewhere deep inside him he felt the gates open and the gushing, surging, billowing fluids raced toward freedom.

"Oh, damn! Oh, damn! Oh, damn," Canyon bellowed as he exploded and plowed deep, and when the last of the urgency had passed, he dropped on top of her, driving Lea deeply into the mattress. Her arms snapped closed around his back and they were locked together.

It was twenty minutes before either of them moved. But not even then could they speak as they lay side by side, her head on his shoulder, her hand on his chest.

He didn't know how long they lay that way. Canyon at last touched her cheek and she turned, watching him in the faint light of the lamp.

"Yes, of course I brought us a midnight snack," Lea said. "Somebody has to think of things like that."

They sat up and she brought out two bottles of wine and apples and crackers and some slabs of cheese.

Lea frowned at Canyon. "You guys sure didn't stop your damn train much today, only once. I've been chasing your train all day. Why the big change in plans?"

"Beyond me, Lea. I just work there. That's good cheese."

"Should be for the price." She laughed. "I hope I can charge it to the paper."

"How is the news writing? Do you enjoy it?"

"Pays the rent until I can marry a rich banker in Kansas City."

"Any prospects?"

"Not yet. How about you?"

"I'm not a rich banker."

"Forget it."

They both laughed.

"How about a tip to a reporter. Is your train going to highball right into Washington, or will you be stopping someplace along the line tomorrow?"

"Can't say. You'll have to ask General Wheeler, he's my boss."

"You're not much help to a working girl."

"I thought I'd been a lot of help. I relieved you of all of your sexual tensions."

Lea laughed. "Not quite all of them. Let's try it again. I'm still tense."

Before morning both of them were exhausted and all tensions were forgotten.

11

Canyon got to the train a half-hour before it was supposed to leave. He'd had a leisurely breakfast and wondered where Wendy was. He decided to meet her at the train. They were set to pull out at six-thirty.

General Wheeler met Canyon at the rear of the train. He waved a piece of paper in one hand and there was terrible fury on his face. He was so angry that he could hardly speak.

"Bastards," he at last bellowed. He held out the paper and Canyon took it and read it. It was printed in large block letters.

Canyon,
We have Wendy Franklin. If the train leaves the station this morning, we'll kill her. The only way you can get her back safe is to come with the president in a light buggy without side curtains. Detailed instructions are below. If you don't come to the place described by ten A.M., Wendy will be used by the ten of us and then used again until she loses her mind. Then we'll kill her. Remember: ten A.M. or you'll never seen Wendy again alive.

Canyon's whole body tightened; his face took on a deadly look that the general had never seen before.

"When did you find this?" Canyon asked.

"Five minutes ago. Somebody put it on the train door."

"Hold the train here. Put all twenty of the troops on duty around the president. I know they've been up all night. Call on the local sheriff and get what help you can. Don't let the president outside the car. Shield that window. I'm going to get Wendy."

"Without the president?"

"Yes. That's a ruse to get him out in the country, where they can assassinate him. Keep him here. Keep the train here. If I'm not back by ten o'clock, haul out of here at top speed and don't stop until you get to Washington."

"But . . . but they said if the train—"

"General, we're talking about two privates here, two soldiers working for you who are expendable. Saving the president's life is what's important. Wendy and I don't count for a damn." Canyon heaved a big sigh and looked away. "Sorry, sir. I forgot there for a minute that I work for you. Those are my suggestions, sir."

"Go," General Wheeler said.

Canyon read through the instructions where to go. The route was simple. He didn't get a buggy. He rented the fastest horse the livery had and a saddle and a Spencer rifle and four full tubes of rounds for quick reloading.

Then he rode. He kept a half-mile away from the route described on the paper, but paralleled it. A mile out of town south, then a half mile east. The meet was to take place at a farmhouse with two windmills, two barns, and a two-story house. It wasn't much different from other farm buildings, except this one had two windmills.

Canyon found the ranch about a half-hour later. The sun was bright and booming up from the horizon. It would be a crisp day. There was no snow here, unusual for February. But the temperature was not much over forty degrees.

Canyon rode down a country road a half-mile from the target farm and saw what he searched for. To the left a line of small trees and brush grew along a creek that meandered through the farmland and came within two hundred yards of the buildings. He rode for the brush line.

He worked slowly forward on the mount screened by the brush until he was as near to the farm as he could get.

Now he tied the horse, took his rifle, and crawled up to the near edge of brush and stared at the farm. He was on the backside of it, with the two barns closest to him.

For a half-hour he watched for any routine. He saw a farmer come out and let out the cows from a small barn and then two horses into a nearby pasture. Then the man returned to the house. A woman left the rear of the house to pump a bucket of water from the well. Canyon saw the shadow of a man standing in the darkness of the kitchen watching the woman through the door.

They were there. The kidnappers were in the house.

Canyon surveyed the place again. He could get to the back of the larger barn and inside through a rear door. But from there to the house was forty yards. No cover, no buildings. Only the well, and that was to the right of the house.

He needed a diversion. He could burn down the small barn. But why should the farmer suffer a loss. He was a victim as well. Then Canyon grinned. He moved so he was screened from the farmhouse, then he sprinted for the back of the big barn. Once there, he paused to catch his breath.

There had been no shouts, no gunfire. Must be that no one had seen him. Good. He eased open the door of the big barn and looked inside. No one there. Lots of hay and stalls for some of the best horses.

He found a pitchfork and forked a stack of hay from the edge of the mow to the rear door. Then he carried the hay outside and to the far side of the barn. When he had a stack six feet high, he decided that was enough. It was twenty feet from the side of the barn, so it was no danger to the building.

He went through to the front wall of the barn and stared at the house through cracks in the boards. Nothing moved. Smoke came from the chimney. It was about 7:30 A.M. Lots of time. He ran to the back of the barn, took out a packet of matches, and pulled two from the wax base and struck them on a rock, then set the pile of hay on fire.

Canyon ran to the nearest corner of the barn and waited. The smoke billowed up and less than a minute later he heard a cry from the house.

"Fire, the barn's on fire!"

He heard someone coming, then a second pair of boot steps slammed his way. He let both the men come around the edge of the barn. One was a farmer in bib overalls and no shirt. He wore a straw hat and stopped when he saw the pile of hay burning.

The second man around the barn was a towner and had out a six-gun. Canyon slammed the side of his 1860 percussion revolver down on the gunman's head and he turned in surprise, then slumped to the ground.

"What in tarnation . . ." the farmer asked.

"Figured you needed some help this morning. How long these people been here?"

"Came last night about midnight. Just walked in and tied up me and my boy and locked my wife in the bedroom. They got a girl with them. She says they kidnapped her. Tall girl with blond hair. Pretty thing.''

"Have they hurt her?"

"Not that I know of. Locked her in the pantry. It don't got no windows."

"How many of them?"

"Four. One in charge has a deep southern accent. They said it should be all over this morning and they wouldn't hurt us if we didn't give them no cause."

"Go back to the front of the barn and yell for some help," Canyon ordered. He had tied up the gunman with his own shoelaces and his neckerchief.

"Can you use that revolver?" the farmer asked.

"I shoot a bit."

The farmer grinned and ran for the side of the barn. He yelled a half-dozen times before he got somebody's attention.

"Send out two or three guys. We got a fire going here, but I think we can stop her," the farmer screamed.

Canyon peered around the edge of the barn from ground level. He saw two men walking toward the barn. That still left one inside.

The men came around the corner of the barn cautiously. They saw the still-burning pile of hay, then their buddy flat on his belly in the ground.

Canyon cocked his six-gun behind them.

"One move, gents, and you both die. Backshooting don't bother me a whit for kidnappers. Both of you, lay down on the ground on your backs . . . now!"

One started to comply, but the other dug for his six-gun. Canyon shot him in the side as he spun around. He jolted back three feet, stumbled, and then fell before his hand could get to the weapon. He shivered, tried to call out, and died.

The other man lifted his hands high. "Don't shoot.

I ain't with them, not really. I just hired on in town last night for five dollars. Didn't say what we were gonna do."

Canyon held his fire. He walked up to the smaller man and took his six-gun from his leather. He thumbed the percussion caps off all five of the gun's cylinders, then gave it back to the man.

"Prove you're not with them. Run back inside and say somehow the farmer got a gun and shot the other two guys. When the man inside believes you, draw down on him, take his gun, and march him outside. Can you do that?"

"As against getting shot? You bet."

"Remember, you can't fire your piece, but he won't know that."

"Yeah, I can bluff real good."

"Go now," Canyon said.

The young man nodded and ran around the side of the barn straight for the house.

Canyon watched him from the side of the barn. For a minute nothing happened. Then there was a shot fired inside the house.

"Who else is in there?" Canyon asked the farmer.

"My sixteen-year-old boy and my wife in the bedroom, and the girl."

"He's going to do something. That young guy is probably dead by now. The last one will try to get out. Run maybe. The guy in there didn't believe the bluff. We've got to wait."

Five minutes later the back door opened, a revolver fired a round toward the barn.

"I'm coming out. You shoot you'll kill the girl. So hold your fire."

Wendy came out. She was wearing the same dress she had on yesterday. The man behind her held his arms around her with the six-gun aimed at the barn.

"You try anything and this one is dead, like we said. You the guy from the train?"

Canyon didn't reply. The man with Wendy walked toward the smaller barn. Canyon figured he was after horses.

"You have riding horses in that barn?" Canyon asked the farmer.

"Yep, two or three of the ones that they brought last night."

Canyon saw that there were no windows or doors on this end of the smaller barn. Once the man went inside he would be blind this way. He waited, not willing to risk a shot at the man for fear of hitting Wendy. A moment later the two went inside the barn and closed the door. Canyon told the farmer to stay where he was and raced for the near side of the small barn.

Inside the barn, the man who held Wendy let her go except for one hand.

"Missie, you stand still when I let go of you. I got to saddle us a horse. You promise that you'll stand still?"

Wendy nodded, her mind working like a whirlwind. What could she do? She had no knife, no gun. He was too big to try to stop him. He'd hit her again if she tried. The barn held half a dozen stalls for horses and two for milk cows. A stack of hay covered one side of the place.

"Girl, I told you to stand still, you hear?"

"Yes, I heard."

The tall man in town clothes scowled at her. He holstered his six-gun and turned. "I been watching you all the time. Don't matter none to me to shoot a woman. You remember that."

Wendy trembled in what she hoped was a proper show of fear. Out of the corner of her eye she had seen a pitchfork stabbed into some hay. If he turned far enough . . .

The man caught up the saddle he had taken off the night before and started to hoist it onto the horse. He blinked as the frightened woman standing near him darted to the left, grabbed something, and spun around.

He faced three shining tines of a pitchfork a foot from his chest.

"Hold on to that saddle, smart guy," Wendy said. "You drop it and this pitchfork goes right into your chest," Wendy snarled.

"What the hell?"

"About where you're headed if you drop that saddle. Now slow and easy, move toward the door. Kick it open with your feet and walk outside slowly."

"Not going to," the tall man said.

Wendy pushed the pitchfork against his chest and jabbed it hard enough to break the skin.

"Hey, damn! You stuck me."

"That's just a sample. Move ahead, slow and easy."

The kidnapper swore softly and walked backward toward the door, bumped it open with his rear end, and backed out of the small barn.

Canyon had made it almost to the door when it suddenly opened and he saw himself staring at the last kidnapper holding a saddle.

Canyon laughed. "Be damned, you captured the big bad kidnapper all by yourself, Wendy."

She glanced at him. Canyon watched Wendy and for a second no one watched the kidnapper. He dropped the saddle. His right hand snaked down for the six-gun still in his leather.

Wendy yelled a warning.

Canyon spun around to face the gunman.

Wendy drove forward with the pitchfork. The middle tine rammed into the gunman's wrist, slanted off a bone, and jabbed out the far side, showing three inches of glistening steel. The tine hit just as the kidnapper lifted the six-gun out of leather. The other two tines went on each side of his wrist. Wendy drove the man's arm back until he howled in pain.

He never did have a firm grasp on the revolver and it fell to the ground.

Canyon let the hammer down on his shooter and pushed it back into the leather holster.

"Wendy Franklin, I don't know why I worried so much about you. If I hadn't come, you'd probably have captured all four of these desperadoes all by yourself."

Wendy's face had gone white. She motioned to the man and pulled the pitchfork out of his arm, then dropped the farm tool/weapon. Canyon grabbed the kidnapper and tied his hands behind him. Then he bound up the puncture wounds on both front and back of the kidnapper's wrist.

Wendy looked away and took a dozen deep breaths. When she came up to Canyon three minutes later, she was almost back to normal.

"This one must have killed the man inside, one of his helpers," Canyon said. "It evidently was a bluff that didn't work. Is the woman all right and the son?"

"Yes, both just scared," Wendy said.

"Did you see where your pitchfork tine went?" Canyon asked Wendy.

She shook her head.

"Right through the middle of a tattoo of a blue goose."

Wendy tried to laugh but it wouldn't come. They got a horse saddled for Wendy, and two for the prisoners.

"As soon as we get to town we'll send the sheriff

out to take your statements and get rid of these two bodies for you,'' Canyon told the farmer.

He nodded his thanks. ''Appreciate your not burning down my barn,'' the farmer said. ''And for rescuing the wife and boy. Thanks again.''

They got back to town just before ten o'clock, and Wendy rode to hold up the train as Canyon turned over the prisoners to the sheriff and filed the complaints.

Twenty minutes later the president's train pulled out of the station with their sights set on Washington, D.C. They would be late getting there, but it was much better than not arriving at all.

Wendy and Canyon sat close together on the train seat. Her hand crept over and caught his.

''I was frightened silly out there today,'' Wendy said. ''I bet you never get afraid.''

Canyon chuckled. ''Don't be ridiculous. Every time I go after somebody with a gun I'm afraid. Men who can fear are the ones who learn how to stay alive. Usually a brave man is just being stupid; he doesn't understand the odds of his surviving, and by some quirk of fate, he comes out alive.''

''I wasn't quite so scared when we got to the barn. Actually, I started thinking clearly and looking for a weapon.''

''You certainly found one. Smartest thing you did was make him hold that saddle. No man can outdraw a three-tined pitchfork when it's an inch from his belly.''

Wendy shivered. ''Hey, if I did it right, then why am I about ready to shake myself to pieces?''

''Letdown,'' Canyon said. ''It was a big emotional experience. You were all keyed up, your blood was pounding and your heart working overtime and your mind racing like a steam engine. Now it's over and things are back to normal, almost. Now your body has to catch up with your mind and it wants to shiver and tremble and maybe let you cry a little. Absolutely normal.''

She turned and watched him. "But . . . but you killed a man out behind the barn. You aren't even sweating.''

"Not my first. Sure, I react. I'm more sorry about the kid who got gunned down than about the older man behind the barn. The kid could have turned around his life if he'd tried. The other guy was in too far, just as good for society that he won't be around to cause trouble.''

"You're tough.''

"Sure.'' He put his arm around her. "Now tremble so I can say I'm comforting you in your time of need.''

"You are, Canyon.''

"Fine. Good thing we had a big breakfast. Doesn't look like we're going to stop now until we need water for the engine.''

12

Lea Jackson planned her last assault on the president's train carefully. She had hoped to find out some information about the train from Canyon, but she had let her passion carry her away and her whole strategy against him had collapsed.

She had been determined that night to tease times and stops from Canyon O'Grady, the security man; and then, when he was limp from his own sexual exhaustion, she would put a knife into his heart and cut down the protection around the president.

Canyon's sexual prowess and her own screaming desires had ruined that plot almost from the start.

Since then, she had worked hard. She had used one of her men to kidnap the girl, hoping that would upset the timetable. It had to a certain extent.

Now she would put her last two efforts into play. A person could only do her best. If it failed, she would know that she had tried to the ultimate.

She had left her last man, Smith, in a small town just across the Pennsylvania boarder. They were far enough ahead of the president's train to set up the operation correctly. If what she heard was accurate, the president's train would roll all the way to Washington, D.C., this day. That would mean it would be dark by the time the cars got into Pennsylvania. Good.

Smith was a farm boy, he should be able to do this

job with no trouble. He had rented a farm wagon at the livery, loaded on half a wagonbox full of red bricks, and then stopped at a sandbar and shoveled the rest of the box full of sand. The wagon and two horses were poised two miles outside of Dumas Center.

Smith knew the timetable. Lea had stopped by at Dumas Center and talked to the stationmaster. Lea explained that she was a journalist for the Kansas City papers and she had been reporting on the president's travels. He had been more than happy to help a pretty young girl. She had bent low over his desk and thought he would climax right there as he looked down the top of her blouse at her two surging breasts.

He had gulped and she stroked his hand and thanked him for the telegraphed schedule for the rest of the president's trip.

President Buchanan should be coming through that small town at a little after seven o'clock tonight. It would be dark by then. Perfect for this try.

Lea rubbed her hand over her forehead. The damn headaches were coming back. She hated them. She didn't know why she had them. Lea sat in a small café in McClarren. It was the same place she had almost bombed the train on its way to Chicago. That time she didn't have the matches. This time it would be different—if her final try at the president was needed. She wondered what Smith was doing in Dumas Center?

Larry Smith sat near his wagon as darkness came down. He had his Waterbury and checked the time. The watch hung on a string tied to the watch on one end and to the belt loop of his pants on the other end. He was proud of the watch. He'd never had one before.

Miss Tits herself had given it to him. He thought about Lea Jackson for a minute. Only once had she let him get her. It was the night she convinced him to come with them on the trip. She had been worth it. Damn, what a sexy woman, small but mighty, and what she could do with her body! He didn't know a female form could bend in so many ways.

He got up and checked the wagon. It was ready. He even had a little downslope to get to the tracks so he'd have no trouble rolling to the rails fast once that sweeper engine roared past. Lea had talked to him for half an hour until he understood the plan. After the engine went past, he'd get the wagon on the tracks.

He'd unhitch the team if there was time. Just pull the pin out of the doubletree and get the horses out of the there. Should be plenty of time.

Smith sat down beside the wagon. Damn heavy load. He had no idea what it would do to the train. Smash it up and throw the cars off the tracks, he guessed. He'd never seen a train wrecked before. Sure somebody would get hurt, but he'd be jogging straightaway from the scene. Might even unhitch one of the horses and ride her away. Yeah, that would be better. If there was time.

Smith shook his head, wondering how he ever got into this deadly little plan that Lea had cooked up. She was weird at times, but she was terrific in bed. She'd promised him that after he got this wagon on the tracks, he'd get another night with her. God damn! Now there was a payoff. Christ, he'd been angling to get her drawers down for a week. God damn!

Down the tracks, less than three miles away, the stationmaster scratched his head as he stood besides the tracks.

"All it says is that they need a spare engine down at Columbus, and we're supposed to send that one we had here waiting to add to that long freight train."

Hugh Nedwiler shook his head. "Damn, wish they

would give me better orders. Do I send it now or wait until after the president's train goes out?''

The engineer lifted his hands in a helpless gesture. "Hell, Hugh, it's your decision. I'm just the train driver.''

"Hell!''

The engineer grinned at the stationmaster. "Just glad it's your decision, not mine,'' the engineer said. "I'll be in the cab when you decide.''

"President's train won't be along for another fifteen minutes. I guess we can clear you here and get you moving down the tracks ahead of them. You got a forty-mile run. Yeah. Okay, get her fired up and out of here.''

The engineer ran to his engine, kicked the fireman awake, and he built a fire in the boiler. It took them almost ten minutes to get up enough steam to move the big engine. Then they chugged out of the station as the boss man on the platform checked his watch and swore.

"Too damn close to the president's rig, but they said do it now, so we send the engine now,'' Hugh said. He kicked a bench on the platform and looked up the tracks, wondering if the president's train would be on time. He had received an updated schedule just this noon.

Larry Smith came off the ground and stared down the tracks toward town. Yeah, he had heard something. Now he could see the light of something. Had to be a train. Yeah, the engine. He got on the wagon seat and checked the brake, letting it off just a fraction of a second. The wagon started to edge forward and he clamped the brake back on.

Might not need the team at all, but he'd use them in

case the rig wouldn't roll all the way to the railroad crossing.

Smith checked his watch. It was maybe ten minutes before seven. The orders said the train would be in the town a little before seven and sweep right on through.

He went over the procedure again. Wait for the engine to come, a single engine that would be right in front of the Presidential Special. Then, when it went past, he would drive onto the tracks, set the brake, unpin that doubletree, and drive the horses away. Then he could unharness one of the nags, jump on board, and ride as far as the horse could go.

Yeah, he had it. Smith turned and watched the light grow larger. Was it a train or just an engine? He couldn't tell yet. Then the sound and the light came closer and he figured by the sound that it was only an engine. Not the clanking and squealing of metal on metal that meant a lot of train cars.

A minute later the big light and the engine hissed and growled and roared past him.

Just an engine. The sweeper engine!

Smith sat there a moment before he realized it was time to act. He grinned, kicked off the wagon brake, and slapped the reins down on the horses' backs.

The slope was enough to get the rig on the tracks. He stopped so his front wheels were right on the far tracks and the rear ones near the back track. The rails were buried in the roadway with ties set long ways to make a smoother crossing.

Larry set the break, jumped down, and threw the reins to the front of the team. He stepped in behind the horses and pulled out the heavy steel pin that held the doubletree attached to the wagon.

"Heeeeeeeeyahhhhhh," Smith bellowed, and the horses moved out, surprised at the lack of weight. The

133

doubletree drug along behind as the horses walked down the dirt road for a quarter of a mile.

Larry didn't wonder where the president's train was. It must have been held up. Hell, he did his part in it just like Lea said to. He could almost feel those soft white thighs of hers and could nearly taste the sweet woman scent of her breasts when he chewed on them.

Far away, maybe down by the town, he heard a train whistle. So it was coming. He turned to watch, then laughed and unharnessed the smaller of the two horses. Quickly he swung up on the animal's back, fashioned a kind of halter, and kicked the mare into motion down the road. Even bareback was lots better than walking.

The sound of the train came closer and he could spot the side of the train engine's light. Didn't seem like it was moving very fast. Not as fast as that other engine. Yeah, going slow, that was why the train was behind the sweeper engine so far.

Smith watched now as the engine came closer. When he figured the engine was fifty yards from the crossing, the big machine started to slow. Then the drive wheels locked and steel ground on steel as the brakes came on. Sparks showered into the night.

Then the engine hit the wagon of bricks. Larry was disappointed. It wasn't a big crash like he had imagined. No explosion, no fire, no grating of steel ripping off tracks.

But it was trouble enough for him. Smith turned the horse parallel with the tracks and rode for town. He'd be on the next regularly scheduled passenger train heading for McClarren, Pennsylvania.

Engineer Pete Petrano thought he saw something ahead in the chilly February night. Something on the tracks. He had slowed at a hundred yards, then at fifty yards he saw the farm wagon in the faint moonlight.

Some damned farmer must have broken down right there.

He hit the brakes, cut power, and the big engine began to slide along the tracks of steel. The wheels screamed in protest, and soon Pete knew he couldn't stop in time.

"Hang on, Joe," Pete bellowed at his fireman.

Then they hit the farm wagon. The pointed cow-catcher on the front of the engine hit first and split the box of the wagon in half, neatly spewing out bricks and sand on each side of the tracks.

A three-foot-high pile of bricks fell between the rails, but the undercarriage of the big engine ground them into brick chips as it slid over them.

"We're gonna stay on the tracks," Pete yelled.

"Damn good," Joe said.

They slid another thirty feet before they came to a stop.

"Take those two red lanterns and get as far down the tracks as you can, Joe. Flag down the train. Don't let it get anywhere near. Got to be a break in the rails or some damage here. I'll get a white lantern and check the tracks.

Joe nodded. "Looks like we at last earned our pay on this sweeper job," Joe said. Then he lit two red railroad lanterns, made sure both had enough kerosene in them, and ran back down the tracks toward the little town and the president's train.

He ran for a hundred yards, then trotted for another hundred. By the time he was five hundred yards from the crash site, he stopped and waited. He couldn't even see the Presidential Special's light yet.

It came five minutes later and his twin waving red lanterns alerted the engineer and he cut speed and eased up to Joe, who stepped to the side, then climbed up into the cab.

Two minutes later Joe told General Wheeler and Canyon what had happened.

"Walk the track ahead of us," General Wheeler ordered Joe, "If you see anything that is damaged, stop us at once. We'll be right behind you, creeping along."

It took them twenty minutes to get to the road crossing and they found no danger. The conductor and both engineers inspected the tracks on and just past the site of the crash. All three said the tracks were safe to use. The wagon had broken up quickly enough and the bricks and sand had scattered, so there was no hard pressure on the drive wheels.

"If he'd had a load of iron pipe in there, we might have been in big trouble," one of the engineers said.

General Wheeler ordered Pete Petrano to back his engine over the suspect tracks. He did without any harm, he backed well beyond the crossing and moved forward again. No problem.

General Wheeler and Canyon watched as the president's train edged forward across the road section and along another fifty yards, then a hundred yards.

"We made it, General," Canyon said.

"By damn, I think we did. I wonder if the Blue Goose Lodge will make another try? We have another four hours before we get into Washington."

"Let's hope that was their last big play," Canyon said. But he didn't believe it. He jumped on the train behind the general, went through the president's car and back to where Wendy waited. He put down the window that she had lifted to watch the proceedings.

"Well, we made it again," Wendy said.

"So far, so good. Only four more hours and this assignment will be done."

Wendy frowned and looked out the window. "Somehow I don't think that will be the last try they make. These people aren't dedicated to their cause, they are fanatic.''

"For the next four hours, Wendy, the two of us must be more fanatic than they are. Are you game?''

Wendy shivered just a moment looking at the stern, deadly expression Canyon wore. Then she nodded. ''Right, only four more hours.''

13

Lea left the café in McClarren and checked with the stationmaster at the depot.

"Yes, miss, nice to see you again. Fact is, I got a message through a few minutes ago. The president's train will be coming in here just after eight o'clock tonight. That puts him another half-hour behind. Sure hope the cook ain't fixed dinner for him in the White House."

Lea laughed and thanked the little man.

"Miss, you know I'm not supposed to say anything about this, but you being a member of the journalism fraternity and all, I figured it was all right."

"It certainly is. I'll have my editor send your boss a thank-you letter." She waved and walked outside. Lea had bought what she needed earlier in the day and now carried her carpetbag, which contained a few clothes and forty pounds of black powder, five feet of fuse, and a stinker plug of matches.

Nothing could go wrong this time.

The train was still coming, only a half-hour behind schedule. That meant Smith had failed when he tried to wreck the president's train with the farm wagon loaded with bricks and sand. Lea thought that would be the one winning play. Somehow Smith had figured out a way to ruin a simple task. She was surrounded by idiots. But then, it was her own fault, she had selected the three men herself.

She walked down the street toward the near end of town to the south. The railroad tracks were only a block over. She would get to them just past the last few houses, maybe a quarter of a mile. She checked a small watch she kept in her reticule. Already it was dark. She lit one of the matches and looked at the watch. Just past seven-thirty. She trudged on, knowing that this would be her last try. She had broken her final twenty-dollar gold piece for her train ticket and supper. It was the last of her hard-earned and scrabble-saved money for the trip. Now she had run out of space and time as well.

Lea angled over through an empty field toward the tracks. There were fewer trees on this side of the ravine than on the other side. But she wouldn't need to hide. She wanted to be close to hear the screams and the pain and wash away her anger and hatred for those terrible men who had killed her father.

She found the tracks and in the darkness picked out the spot. She would put the powder on top of the tie, six feet out on the trestle-type bridge. She packed the four small sacks next to each other on the tie and right next to the outside of the rail on the right side.

The slope down the right-of-way was more gradual here and she would want to get away far enough to be safe. When she had the sacks of black powder in place, she used baling wire to lash the powder in place, running the wire around the tie and up on the other side, then twisting the ends until her fingers hurt. Now the vibrations of the train would not knock the bomb off the track.

She cut a length of fuse two feet long, pushed it in a hole in the middle sack of powder. That would give her two minutes to get off the bridge and out of the danger area. She looked at it, then made another fuse only five inches long. She pushed this one until only three inches remained out of the bomb. That would be her emergency fuse.

If the short fuse burned as fast as it did sometimes, she would be blown up with the bomb. Hoisted by her own petard. Lea shrugged. That was only if she had to use it. Timing was important. The bomb had to go off just before the train got to the bridge, but not so quickly that they could stop it before plunging into the one-hundred-foot ravine.

She stared into the darkness of the hole, then walked back to the ground and sat beside the tracks waiting. She would use three matches together as she struck them on the rail. Then, if one did not strike, the second or third would. Yes. No damn mistakes this time.

For you, Daddy. I'm doing this all for you. Then maybe your poor screaming soul can rest in peace.

Lea lit a match on the rail, practicing. By the light she checked her watch. Fifteen minutes until eight. She walked out on the bridge and sat beside the bomb. She knew just how many ties it was back to the land. She carried the three matches in her hand, careful not to get the sulfur ends damp by her own sweat.

Lea looked up and down the tracks but could see nothing. She put her ear on the steel rail. There was only a soft humming sound. Not the grinding, rolling sound of a rain, which could be heard miles away through the tracks.

Time dragged by. She wanted to look at her watch again, but there was no need. When the train came, she would be ready. Until then, she would wait patiently. This time everything would go right and President Buchanan would die!

They would send the single engine ahead of the main train. She knew that, which meant she did have to hide until it had passed. Then she might have to scramble quickly to the bridge. She retreated to the right-of-way and found a place where she could crouch low to the ground like a big rock. The lights on the engines weren't that good. Yes, that would work. She sat there waiting, knowing that this was the time everything worked right.

On the Presidential Special, Wendy and Canyon sat close together in the darkened car. Most of the soldiers ahead were sleeping. The pair had been talking ever since they got back on the train. She had lost her shivering.

Canyon put his arm around her and held her.

Wendy sighed and leaned against him. "In a way I'm going to be sad when this assignment is over," she said.

"Me too. We'll be off on other missions, separate ones anywhere in the country. I might not see you again for six months or more."

"You must! I'll give you the address of the boardinghouse where I stay when I'm in Washington. I moved from my father's house a year ago." She lifted her face and kissed his cheek. "Canyon?"

He smiled, turned, and kissed her lips, a light, friendly kiss.

She murmured deep in her throat when he pulled away. "That wasn't exactly what I had in mind, Canyon O'Grady," she whispered.

"Well, now." He bent and kissed her again, and this time it was hot and hard and demanding. She went with the kiss, and when it was over, she smiled at him in the near darkness and then reached up and pulled down his head and kissed him again. Her tongue darted into his mouth and then back again and she moaned softly.

They parted and she smiled at him. "Thank you, nice Canyon O'Grady," she whispered again. Then she took his hand and put it over one of her breasts and reached up and kissed him once more. When they parted, she sighed softly and looked up at him in the faint light.

"Yes, Canyon O'Grady, that was more what I had in mind," she whispered.

"Does the train stop again?" Canyon asked.

"I heard the conductor talking a half-hour ago. He said we need to stop in McClarren for water. The engineer says he's running low."

Canyon kissed her again and his hand caressed her breast through the blouse and light jacket she wore.

"If we had time, I'd be tempted to undress you right here," he whispered.

She hit his arm with her hand. "That is naughty. You would not do such a thing." She smiled, feeling his hand working through the buttons on her blouse. "I really don't mind your hand moving around a little though."

"I hoped that you wouldn't."

Someone came down the aisle and they closed their eyes and pretended to be sleeping side by side. When the steps passed, they looked up, grinning like a pair of conspirators.

Canyon kissed her again, and this time her lips opened. He found the secret and worked his hand under her chemise and up to one softly round, bare breast.

Wendy's eyes went wide. "Oh, my! Mr. O'Grady, I do think you're trying to seduce me."

"Wonderful idea, but unfortunately this is the wrong place, wrong time." He kissed her again then, just as they felt the train slow down.

"Oh, damn," Canyon whispered. "We must be to McClarren. Some of the worst timing I've ever seen."

The conductor came through and Canyon pulled his hand away from her and they eased apart. He saw them awake and nodded. "We're making a stop for water, folks. This is McClarren, Pennsylvania. We'll be here about twenty minutes. We need to take on some more wood as well. Sorry for the inconvenience, but we'll get moving as soon as we can."

"Twenty minutes," Canyon said. "Let's go for a walk. Lots of time. Isn't this the place that has that bridge, the one over a gully of some kind?"

"Yes, a deep gully, more than a hundred feet it says on my map."

"You have good maps. Let's go take a look at the bridge and see if it's still standing."

They walked down the street next to the tracks. They had passed the sweep engine that stopped just beyond the water tower. When they were on the far side of a house with lights that glowed into the street, they stopped and kissed.

"Hey, it works standing up," Wendy said.

They laughed and continued on.

"Best field assignment I've ever been on," Wendy said with a little sigh.

"That was easy, lady agent. This is your very first fieldwork."

"I know, and the best. The next one won't be nearly so exciting, or nice." She put her arm through his and they kept walking.

"Why are we coming out here three or four blocks to look at the bridge?" Wendy said.

"Just a feeling I have," Canyon said. "Anyway, it was a good place to kiss you."

They stopped in the darkness and their lips melted together and mouths opened and he felt his blood starting to race through his veins twice as fast as usual. Wendy gave a soft little cry and her arms came around him so tightly he grunted.

When they finally broke the kiss, he held her close, her breasts hard against his chest.

"Wendy Franklin, you shouldn't kiss a man that way unless you really mean it."

"I really mean it. How much time do we have?"

"You're serious?"

"Absolutely, I'm serious. Right here and right now," she said, hugging him again.

"Not nearly enough time. No, Miss Franklin. When we make love, it's going to be in a beautiful room with wine and a big soft bed, and we're going to do it right. Not like a couple of kids behind the barn."

"Oh, damn." She punched him on the arm. "Race you to the bridge, then we can get back to the train and snuggle all the way to Washington." She turned and ran toward the bridge.

Canyon hurried after her. It was only a short way then. They stood at the spot where the tracks marched out onto the wooden platform of the bridge and looked at it.

"Hope it holds up for one more trip," Wendy said.

"It did the last time. I'll walk out on it just to show you."

Before he could, they heard the sweeper engine coming. It had its light on and ground down the tracks, not yet up to speed, but starting to roll.

"That means the president's train is going to leave in a couple of minutes," Canyon yelled. He caught Wendy and tugged her down off the tracks on the right of way and watched as the sweeper engine plowed past them, hissing and steaming.

"We'll never get back in time to catch the train," Wendy said.

"So, we'll get the next one. I still want to take a look at this bridge."

"The sweeper engine got across with no trouble," Wendy said. "Look, you can still see the red lantern on the back of it."

"I'm taking a look." Canyon ran up the side of the right-of-way to the tracks and down twenty yards to the edge of the bridge. He walked out six or eight feet, and before he could go farther, a shot sliced through the night and the bullet missed him but made him pull back to the far side of the mound of dirt the tracks had been laid on.

Wendy was on the other side of the tracks now, the same side where the gunman was.

"Stay there, Wendy," Canyon called. He had out his own weapon now, and he slid up to the edge of the tracks, trying to see in the darkness ahead of him. He was fifty feet from the start of the bridge.

Clouds swept over the moon and he couldn't see a dozen feet ahead. Shadows formed and wavered and melted into the blackness. Had he seen a body moving on the tracks? Which way? Yes, went out on the bridge. Who?

He edged closer along the steel rails, then he did see a figure. Someone darted back from the bridge and jumped off the tracks and down the far side and vanished. Why? Only one reason: to plant something on the tracks to stop the president and maybe wreck the train.

Then the reality of it came. Whoever it was had waited for the sweeper train to come by. Now Canyon could feel and hear the president's train moving down the tracks. He hadn't noticed it before.

He turned and saw the big light on the front of the engine. Coming! It was coming. He sniffed. Something. What? He sniffed again.

A black powder fuse, a bomb fuse. On the bridge. Canyon turned now and ran down toward the bridge. It was so dark.

He got to within a dozen feet of the start of the wooden structure and he saw it, a bomb fuse sputtering on the right-hand side of the track. A bomb and the fuse lit and burning. If it burned for another minute it would blow up just about the time the president's train got there.

Yank out the damn fuse!

Canyon lifted up and ran, pounding on the ties, hitting every other one until he saw no dirt below them, then he slowed. The fuse sputtered ahead. He saw it coming up and bent lower so whoever had lit it might not see him.

Now he could see clearly the fuse sputtering, and in the faint light that fire made, he saw sacks packed and tied next to the rail.

It was a big bomb, plenty of powder to blow that end of the bridge fifty yards up the ravine.

Canyon bent low and started out on the bridge. Close by, a revolver snarled in the blackness. A huge fist hit Canyon in the thigh and levered him backward. He grabbed the steel rail with both hands as his legs dangled over the edge of the bridge. He had no idea how far it was to solid ground below him.

The pain was like the engine had just cut his leg off. It took him three tries to swing his legs back up on the ties. Then he crawled toward the bomb.

The hand gun spoke again and then once more in well-spaced shots that slammed between him and the bomb, sending him a message. If he went forward, the faint light of the sputtering fuse would outline him and he would be a dead man. If he didn't surge up there and pull the fuse, the bridge would blow and the president could die.

The train kept coming forward. He could hear the wheels grinding on the rails now. He looked at the bomb, then back at the train.

He had to try for the bomb.

Canyon lifted up and started to move forward. Just then Wendy dropped onto the ties beside him.

"I saw where those shots came from, let me try to draw his fire."

Wendy had out the big .41-caliber solid-cartridge revolver. She fired once down the side of the embankment, then again.

Below, the revolver returned fire but missed them by six feet.

"Four, whoever it is has fired four times," Canyon said. "He must only have one round left. I'm heading out there."

"No, wait, let me get that last round from him." Wendy moved back along the tracks six feet and fired twice more at the bomber, then rolled twice. The final round from the hidden revolver came and missed. Canyon O'Grady lifted up and stared at the bright-yellow light of the train heading toward him. It was still fifty yards away. Lots of time, Canyon thought as he raced toward the bomb.

Lots of time for the train, but how short was that damn fuse going into the bomb?

14

Canyon ran down the tracks toward the bomb. He could see the fuse burning. How long was the fuse? How much time did he have? He had to try for it. It could be the last thing he ever did. At least whoever was firing wouldn't be able to reload a percussion revolver quickly in the dark.

For a minute he wondered what if it wasn't a percussion, or what if the guy had two revolvers. Then he put that out of mind.

Run!

He hit the bridge and just then a booming roar came as a shotgun went off. Canyon heard the slugs hitting the bank and the rails. Something tore at his pants leg and then he was through the hail of double-aught buck. It had to be the big slugs by the sound on the rails.

He heard Wendy firing behind him and realized she had reloaded with her solid rounds.

Then he had no time to think because he could see the fuse sputtering just ahead of him. He dived to the steel rail, hit it on his chest, and his right hand darted out and grabbed the sputtering fuse and jerked it out.

The pain in his hand came immediately and was excruciating. He tried to drop the fuse but it was burned into his hand. He tightened his fist harder and put out the burning, then he rolled over and looked at the bomb. Four sacks of powder. He took a match from his pocket and struck it and in the quick light saw that there was another fuse sticking from the bomb, but it was unlit. He pulled it out, then turned and stared at the train.

Canyon saw the train almost on top of him. There was no time to run off the bridge. He swung over the side and held on to the ties, then his legs wrapped around one of the vertical supports and he hung on like a monkey.

The charging president's three-car train slammed across the bridge at thirty miles an hour, hissing and grinding and churning. A shower of sparks and steam and then hot water splashed down on him and four seconds later the last car blasted past him.

Canyon hung there a moment, then he saw cross braces on the bridge just under the rails. He let go of the ties, hugged the vertical support beam, and lowered down to the cross brace. His left leg burned like fire. The round that hit him in the leg must not have hit a bone. Probably went on through. He could feel blood running down his leg. How much was he bleeding? First, he had to get off the bridge.

From the cross brace, he worked back to the embankment, climbed up the rocks and dirt to the rails, and sat there a moment panting. His leg became one big throbbing pain. He wasn't sure if he could walk.

But he could. He heard Wendy fire twice more as he limped down the right-of-way on the side across from the shotgun.

Wendy watched Canyon run toward the burning fuse. She was sure she knew where the gunman was ahead. She put down covering fire for Canyon even though she didn't think the gunman ahead had had time to reload.

She fired the last shots from her revolver, then

quickly reloaded the solid rounds as she had practiced in the dark. She put in six rounds and snapped the weapon together and watched her target. There had been no return fire at her since that first one.

She leveled in on the suspected area and fired one more round. As the sound echoed away, she heard a cry of pain, then she heard a booming roar of a shotgun and Wendy screamed at the gunman.

She fired the last five shots from her weapon at and around the muzzle flash of the shotgun. She knew what a scattergun could do, especially with a double-aught shot.

Tears streaked down her cheeks as she rammed the brass out of her revolver and reloaded it again. There had been no second blast of the shotgun.

Good, maybe I wounded him so he can't shoot anymore.

She lay there waiting. The cold steel of the rail pressed against her arm. She was between the rails so she had some protection from the gunman.

Now Wendy looked forward at where Canyon had vanished in the darkness. She had heard nothing. There was no soft glow of the burning fuse she had seen before. There had been no explosion. Maybe Canyon had got there in time to pull out the fuse.

Wendy felt as much as heard the train coming from behind her. She rolled off the tracks and down the embankment on the shotgunner's side. The train had been within fifty feet of her and now slammed past. She hadn't realized a train made that much noise.

When the noise faded, it was as quiet as a winter night in Pennsylvania. The cold now nipped at her nose. She lay still, six rounds in her weapon. She had it cocked and ready.

A sound came from across the tracks away from the shotgunner.

Wendy swung around her revolver up and waiting. She saw a shadow at the top of the embankment in the dark and her finger began to tighten on the trigger.

"Wendy," Canyon said.

"Oh, God!" She let out a long held-in breath. "Down here. God, I almost shot you." She lowered the weapon and aimed it away from him.

"Did you get the bomb?"

Canyon slipped down the embankment and sat beside her in the grass and weeds. "Yes, the bomb is dead. What about that outlaw with the shotgun?"

"Haven't heard a thing since that last shot."

"We have to go up there and find him. He could get away by morning. We have to finish this once and for all tonight." He sat beside her and fumbled in his pockets. "You ever reloaded a percussion revolver?"

"Yes, in the daylight."

"I need some help."

"Oh! Did that shotgun hit you?"

"No, just a burn on my hand, but it doesn't function well. I'll get the linen cartridges punched in the chambers if you can put on the percussion caps on the nipples."

They worked at it for almost four minutes. She dropped three of the small percussion caps before she had the six firmly in place.

Canyon kissed her cheek. "Thanks, now I'm going up there and find that shotgunner."

"I'm going with you."

He watched her in the darkness. "You earned the right. We'll work up on this side quietly for a bit. When we move forward, we stay ten feet apart, so one lucky blast of that scattergun won't chop us both to bits."

"I've got it. Let's go."

They moved cautiously forward ten yards, then knelt

down and waited. Nothing happened. Canyon motioned her to move to one side five yards and they began walking forward cautiously.

Canyon made no noise at all. He could hear her moving, but when he stopped to listen, he could hear no sound from where the gunman must be. A nighthawk let out a piercing cry, then there was the silence of winter's darkness.

Canyon paused in the black night and knelt. He didn't like it. Whoever was up there was playing it very smart—or he was dead. But which? Canyon lifted his six-gun, aimed at the spot he figured the gunman would be, and fired, then he dived to the left behind a large rock that had been rolled aside from the grading of the right-of-way.

Within two seconds, the shotgun roared again, the double-aught buck stripping and tearing up the ground and small bushes where Canyon had been moments before.

Almost on top of that sound came two quick shots from the left. That had to be Wendy. The gunner could still have another round in the shotgun. As Canyon thought about it, the shotgun went off again, but this time unaimed or in the air.

The sound was followed by a long wailing cry of pain and frustration.

Now!

His shotgun was out of rounds, six-gun dry. Do it! Canyon jumped up and charged the last ten yards at the clump of bushes. He crashed through and stopped, his six-gun ready.

The moon had come out and now he could see the person who lay on the ground in front of him. The figure held a sawed-off shotgun, but the hand was not on the trigger.

Canyon leapt in, grabbed the shotgun and a revolver. That's when he realized the gunman was a woman. She sat upright now, her hands holding her belly. She wore a dress and a hat. She had a carpetbag nearby that was large enough to hold the cut-off shotgun.

"It's over, Wendy," Canyon said softly.

Wendy came in, her weapon still ready. She knelt down in front of the woman and looked at Canyon in surprise. "A woman?"

The shooter's face came up and she glared at Wendy. "And so what if I'm a woman? I was shot twice, but I was waiting to take you both out with my shotgun. Then those last two rounds caught me in the belly. You gut-shot me."

Her voice had been strong, but it grew weaker as she finished the tirade.

"Why not a woman? Northerners killed my pa down in Kansas. Bloody John Brown did it for no reason at all except Pa came from Tennessee. Damn him. Damn all of you damn northerners."

"So you were going to kill the president to get even," Canyon said. He thought he recognized the voice. He bent to see her short black hair.

"Yes. I would have done it, just a few more seconds and that fuse would have hit the powder."

"Do you have a blue goose tattooed on your right wrist?" Canyon asked. He thought again that he should know the voice. He listened closely.

"Yes, I have the blue goose. God, that hurts! I've heard being shot in the belly is the worst way there is to die."

Then Canyon had it. "Was the newspaper reporter just a screen of thick smoke to hide behind while you did your dirty work, Lea Jackson?"

"No. I am a reporter for the newspaper. I just hadn't sent them anything for a month."

153

Wendy frowned. "You've seen this woman before?"

"Twice. She claimed to be a reporter, even had a letter from the publisher. But it was only to mislead us."

"You going to get me to a doctor?" Lea asked.

"Won't do any good," Wendy said. "You must know that. A doctor could only give you some laudanum. Maybe someday the doctors will figure out how to save somebody gut-shot, but not so far."

"Moving you would cause you so much pain you'd ask us to stop," Canyon said.

"You've killed men before this way, Canyon?"

He hesitated. Wendy looked at him in the dim light. "Yes," he said.

"Could you start a fire? I'm cold."

Canyon gathered dry twigs and branches from the nearby trees, cleared a space, and started a small fire. Lea huddled near the flames, warming her hands. Not moving much. Each time she moved her torso or legs, she screamed in pain.

Twice she shrilled in agony as the rumbles of pain drilled through her.

Canyon whispered to Wendy. "You can go back to town. You don't have to watch this."

Wendy whispered back. "I shot her, I must at least watch her die."

Lea looked at them. "No secrets. You won, I lost, now I'm going to die. I've heard how bad it can be. Please don't leave me here alone."

"We won't," Wendy said, tears brimming her eyes. "Why did you do all of this?"

"Told you. John Brown hacked my father to death for no reason at all, just because he favored slaves for Kansas. I've been waiting for my revenge ever since."

"And you were willing to sacrifice thirty people's lives so you could kill the president?"

"Three hundred of you northerners, if it came to that. It was all James Buchanan's fault in the first place." She screamed again, reached out for Wendy, who caught her shoulders as the agony of pain tore through Lea, shaking her.

"Oh, God! You didn't say it would be this bad. If I could have seen to load my revolver, I'd have saved one shot for myself."

"Talk to me about the good times," Wendy said. "Remember the very best day of your life. What did you do? What happened? Tell me about it."

"Why, so you can gloat?"

"No, Lea, so you'll be thinking good things and it'll make you feel better. Try it. What day was the very best for you?"

Lea began then in a thin voice, remembering her childhood and the best time when her father brought her a pony and taught her to ride. Then she talked about school and a church picnic. The pain came more often now and she screamed sometimes, but more often she simply tightened up and rode through it gritting her teeth and closing her eyes.

Her voice got softer and softer. She moved closer to the fire and brayed in pain. At last she lay down with her head in Wendy's lap. That eased the agony a little.

She went on talking and her voice became softer and softer. She was in the middle of a story about her first Easter egg hunt when she stopped talking, then started again. Then she stopped and a rush of air came from her lungs and her head turned slowly to the side. Her sightless eyes stared at Wendy in accusation.

They left her there beside the tracks. Canyon went back to the bridge and unwrapped the wire and took away the four sacks of black powder. He cut the sacks and let the powder fall out into the brush where it would be harmless.

Then they walked back toward the railroad station. Canyon tried not to let his limp show.

"We'll catch the late train. I saw that there's one leaving here about nine o'clock tonight, which should put us in Washington around midnight."

Suddenly Wendy leaned against him. Canyon stopped and looked at her. Tears streamed down her cheeks, then she was sobbing.

"I killed her. I killed that poor girl. She didn't look any older than I am, and I shot her down."

Canyon put his arms around her and they stood there in the middle of the street in a small Pennsylvania town as Wendy cried her heart out. He held her gently and she sobbed against his chest. His leg burned and growled with pain. He could feel blood now squishing in his boot where it had run down his leg.

"No older than I am and she's dead. I shot her. I'm a killer. I never intended to kill her. I saw her fire that shotgun toward where I knew you were, and I got scared and I fired six times as fast as I could." She sobbed again. Then she said something else, but she was crying so hard he couldn't understand her.

Canyon turned her, held her tightly, and took a step toward the train station and then another. Slowly she began to walk with him. He gritted his teeth and walked over the pain in his leg.

"Never . . . meant . . . to . . . kill . . . her."

"I know, I know, Franklin. It happens. I'm just glad that it's her and not you lying back there in the grass. Remember, anyone who picks up a gun and shoots at somebody is trying to kill that person. When that happens, the shooter must be ready to die as well. The shooter becomes a target, a legitimate threat to life and a candidate for death herself."

"I killed her."

They walked another block and the sobbing stopped.

It was replaced by big gasps for air and shivering. The pain in his leg had eased off to a dull throbbing fury.

"I'll never pick up a firearm again. I'm quitting the agency. I'll never shoot at anybody, not ever again."

"Give it some time, Franklin. Now you see the tough side of fieldwork. It's not all fun and frolic out here. You need to give it some time."

"It won't matter. I'll never go on another assignment."

She didn't say anything the last two blocks to the train station. Inside, Canyon bought two tickets to Washington. The train would be along at 9:10 P.M.

Canyon and Wendy sat on a bench inside the heated station. She still shivered. He put his arm around her and held her close, but it didn't help.

"Wendy, did I tell you about the first time I had to kill a man?"

"I don't want to know about it."

He went on as if he didn't hear her. "It was an assignment out of Omaha. A government official had been killed out there and I had to find out who and why. When I finally untangled the mess the man had made of his life and got down to the cause of his death, I found the man responsible.

"He was a cheat, a scoundrel. He had killed three men by that time and was about to shoot a woman. He drew down on me and we both fired; he missed but I didn't. No man deserved to die any more than he did.

"After the man fell and died, I dropped my six-gun and walked into the prairie. I walked all night, and when morning came, I was twenty miles from the little town. I still hadn't accepted the idea that I had killed this guy. I turned and started back to town and the local sheriff met me about half an hour later.

"He came looking for me, leading a horse behind his own. He talked all the way back to town. He at last convinced me that I had done the right thing. If that man hadn't died, he would have gone on cheating and killing others. He told me I had only done my job. I had only done my job. But besides that, I had done a great service to the community. I had saved lives.

"Wendy, how many lives do you think you saved today by pinning down Lea so I could get to that bomb?"

She looked at him, frowned, but said nothing.

"If you hadn't fired at her when you did, I never would have been able to get to the bomb. It would have gone off about fifty feet before the train got there and at least half, and maybe everyone on board would have died, me included. Without us, there were twenty-eight human beings on that train."

Wendy blinked. For a moment he saw reason return to her eyes, then it vanished. He touched her face with his right hand and she pulled away and stared at it.

"You're hurt," Wendy said. "Your hand is burned. The fuse is stuck in your flesh." She stood and hurried to the ticket-seller and talked a moment, then came back.

"That man is bringing some whiskey and some bandages and a sharp knife. We have to treat your hand before it gets infected."

She held his hand and stared at it. The burned fuse made a nasty two-inch mark on his palm, below that was another inch of unburned fuse.

"You. . . . you pulled the fuse out only a few seconds before it would have exploded. You were almost killed."

"Almost doesn't count in an explosion," he said.

She looked at him again and saw the blood on his left thigh pants leg.

"Oh, you're shot, too. Why didn't you tell me?"

The ticket-seller came then with a kit of bandages,

scissors, a knife, some ointment, and a flask of whiskey.

"My old doctor used to splash whiskey on a wound," the man said. "Don't know why and it hurt like hell, but he said it made it heal better."

The key began to chatter and the railroad man lay down the goods and hurried back to the telegraph.

Wendy stared at Canyon, then took the scissors and knife. "We'll fix you up first, Canyon O'Grady. Then we'll worry about how to handle me and my problem."

She touched the unburned part of the fuse and Canyon winced. Yes, he told himself. Wendy was going to be all right. She just needed some time.

15

Wendy worked quickly and efficiently. She used the thin scissors to cut the black powder fuse away from the dead burned skin and take it off Canyon's hand. Then in the station office she soaked his hand in cold water for a half-hour as she treated his leg.

The bullet had gone all the way through his leg, but he hadn't bled as much as he thought. She put a bandage on it, wrapped it tightly, and he pulled up his pants. She hadn't been embarrassed at all when she told him to pull down his pants so she could get to the wound.

When his hand came out of the cold water, he said it felt a hundred times better. She soothed on some ointment and then bandaged the ugly burn across his palm.

They caught the eastbound 9:10 and settled down in a seat.

Wendy looked at Canyon. "I killed that woman tonight. I didn't mean to, but I killed her. But you said when I did I allowed you time to get to the bomb and pull out the fuse." She frowned for a minute. "So you said I saved the lives of maybe fifteen or twenty people, including yours."

Wendy looked at him and he started to say something but she put a finger across his lips. "No, let me talk it out. I'm in stage two now, I think. I'm through crying and being gushy and emotional. Now I need to work it out on a logical basis. Do you understand?''

Canyon nodded. He listened to her talk for nearly a half-hour. By then, her voice was growing hoarse and she leaned against him. When he looked down at her, she smiled.

"At the next stop let's see if we can buy some sandwiches and some apples or something. I'm starved to death.''

Canyon nodded. She had made it. Wendy would be all right.

They found some food and arrived in Washington a half-hour late at 12:35 A.M. Canyon woke up a cabby and he took them to Wendy's boardinghouse, where she kissed him good-bye, and then the hack drove him to his residence hotel not far from the White House.

They had arranged to meet at a café nearby for breakfast at eight-thirty that same morning. It wasn't long for them to sleep, but they had to be at the White House by ten o'clock.

Breakfast was mostly talk. Wendy wore a bright spring dress and a warm jacket to fend off Washington's chilly winter day. She was bright and sparkling, and after five minutes, Canyon reached over and took her hand. 'You're trying to be a little too casual, too unaffected. Remember the rest of us understand. We've been there. Just relax and act normal and it will be fine.

"Too much, I guess. I really came to grips with it last night on that train ride. Don't worry, I'm not quitting as an agent. I have accepted the dangers of the job, and I think I'm more ready for them now than I was yesterday.''

"Good, let's go see the boss.''

They met as usual in General Wheeler's office in the lower level of the White House. He was waiting for them. He watched Wendy for a moment. Canyon briefed him on what happened.

"General Wheeler, I'm fine," she said quickly. "Canyon and I had a long talk last night on the train and we worked it out. . . . I worked it out. I'm not quitting and I'll be able to use my weapons again if the need arises."

"Good, good. I know there was some concern. From what Canyon just told me, we're putting you in for a special presidential citation. A lot of us on that train owe our lives to you, young lady, and we want to make sure that you get the recognition you deserve." He stood up. "Now, it's time for us to go in and see the president. I think he's glad to be back from the trip."

President Buchanan welcomed them with cups of hot spiced tea, small cakes, handshakes, and a hug for Wendy. General Wheeler briefed the president on what happened at the McClarren Bridge.

"Now, first let me say this. All of us on that train owe you two a lot. I'm making out citations and striking a medal for each of you. If it wasn't for you two, a lot of us on the train would have been dead by now.

"Next, within this room I'll admit that I was an old fool, stubborn and not too smart by insisting on the train trip and all of the stops. You folks were right and I was wrong. Now that we have that out of the way, have some tea. These cakes are delightful."

The president looked at Wendy. "Young lady, how are you doing? You had a difficult job last night, but you performed like a veteran."

"Mr. President, I worked it out and everything is fine now. I'm looking forward to my next assignment."

"Fine, fine. You know I won't be around much longer. I've set it up so all three of you are government employees and automatically remain on the payroll and are on call by the new president, Mr. Lincoln. I hope that he uses you, and I'll explain to him your duties and the fine job that the special agents have done.''

A man came in the side door and cleared his throat. The president looked at him. "Two minutes before the ambassador is due, Mr. President. He's in the lobby now.''

"Yes, yes. Thank you, Robert. Duty calls. Oh, one last item. Both of you are being given a week of vacation time. I want you to enjoy yourselves for a week and rest up, and you heal up, Canyon. I may have one more problem for you before the inauguration of Mr. Lincoln March fourth. More than three weeks away. We shall see. Now, I thank you all for coming.''

The three of them filed out to the hall and back to General Wheeler's office.

"Well, now, a week without a solitary thing to do,'' General Wheeler said. "That means I don't want to see either of you until a week from today, nine o'clock right here. We'll find out what else the president has planned.''

They said good-bye and walked out into the bright sunshine of the winter morning.

"First, Canyon O'Grady," Wendy said, "I'm taking you to a good doctor to have some professional work on your hand and your leg. Then we're going to your residence hotel and talk things over.''

Canyon looked at her with surprise. "You're coming up to my hotel room?'

"Absolutely. You don't think that since I've come so close to knowing what making love is all about, I'm going to pass up my chance now, do you?''

Canyon grinned. "Dear God, I was hoping you wouldn't.''

She hit him on the arm and they hurried to find a

cab to take them to the government doctor they used when they were in town.

An hour later, Canyon O'Grady sat on the edge of the bed in his room beside Wendy. He had just kissed her and she had opened her eyes lazily and then smiled.

"You said it would be in a room with a big bed," she murmured. "I'd say this is the right place."

He caught her chin with his thumb and finger and she looked at him. "Wendy Franklin, you're sure? You know that, once done, there's no reversal, no going back, no starting over."

"I've considered that. I even know that you don't have the slightest intention of marrying me. I don't want to get married right now, either. And yes, Canyon O'Grady, I'm damn sure."

They both chuckled and he kissed her softly, so gently that for a moment she wasn't sure his lips had touched hers.

"Canyon, you know that drives me absolutely wild." She caught him and leaned in front of him and pushed him down on the bed. She fell on top of him, her soft breasts pushing against his face.

She rolled off him and came back close. His arm went around her and she snuggled against him.

"Canyon O'Grady, will I like making love?"

"Do you like my kissing you?"

"Oh, yes."

"Did you like it when my hand was on your bare breast?"

"It was wonderful, like no feeling I've ever had before."

"Then you love making love. That bare breast is a good place to start." His hands worked at the buttons down the front of her dress, then at the chemise, and a moment later his hand rested on her bare breast, which was hot already and pounding and filled with new blood.

Softly he caressed her breast, working up to the peak, rolling her nipple between his thumb and finger, then tracing its outline.

He pushed back her dress and chemise and anointed her other breast the same way, then he bent and kissed one.

"Oh, my, Canyon! Yes. That's the most thrilling . . ."

He kissed her other breast, then sucked her nipple into his mouth and tongued it, then nibbled at it with his gentle teeth.

"Oh, God! Canyon! Oh, yes . . . fine . . ."

He pulled her up to a sitting position and pushed the dress off her shoulders and she lifted the chemise over her head. Her breasts were solid and large, with soft pink areolaes and deeper red nipples now standing tall.

"Put your hands back on me, Canyon. I want your hands on my skin. I love your touch."

He took one of her hands first and put it over his fly so she could feel the hardness there.

"Oh, my," she said softly. She kissed him and wound her tongue around his mouth. They came apart a moment later and he bent and sucked half of one of her orbs into his mouth, chewing on her tenderly.

Wendy growled deep in her throat. She moaned for a moment, then her hand worked at undoing his fly buttons.

Canyon came away from her and they both stood. She lifted the dress over her head, then two petticoats, and she stood before him in the Washington afternoon wearing only a pair of white cotton drawers, tight on the leg down to her knees. It had small ruffles and tiny blue and pink ribbons.

He smiled and she tugged at his belt, and a moment

later she had taken down his pants. He sat and pulled off his boots and his pants and then he stripped out of his shirt and light cotton undershirt.

They both lay down again, she playing with the red hair on his chest, he fondling her breasts, caressing them, listening to her breathing, which rushed faster and faster.

Canyon watched the way her blond hair kept getting in the way. She pushed it back, then let it fall forward, completely covering her breasts.

Wendy turned to him, her face serious. "Canyon O'Grady, you show me what to do."

He laughed softly and kissed her. "There's nothing complicated about making love. You'll know exactly what to do. Do anything you feel like. This is the day to let down all of your reserves. Don't worry about your dress slipping up and showing your ankle or how much breast shows through a dress. Do whatever you want to."

She smiled and moved her hands to his crotch, pulled open his short undergarment, and swung up his manhood. Wendy gasped.

"Oh, my goodness! So big, so beautiful." She let her hand touch the point of him, then slide down the length. "I've never seen . . ." She stopped. Her hands found his pulled-up tight scrotum and she fingered it a moment, then grasped his rod and smiled. "This is what they really mean when they talk about the staff of life."

She bent and kissed him then, and her breath came in surges. His hands worked down across her flat belly to the drawers. Quickly she unbuttoned the side and he edged them down. For a moment her hands caught his and she held them, then she sighed.

"Yes, darling, Canyon. Please, take them off me. I want to know. I want to experience it now."

He stripped down the cotton drawers and pulled them off her legs. Her fluff of blond muff lifted after its confinement.

He threw the drawers on the floor and pushed her down gently on her back, then kissed both flattened breasts and trailed a hot line of kisses down her flat belly toward her small mound over her tangle of blond hair.

"Canyon, I'm going to explode," she said. "I've never felt this way." His hand entered the blond fur and she jolted and shivered and then rattled as her body shook and shook from the spasms of a hard climax. She moaned and her voice rose into a high shriek of pleasure and then died, and she moaned again as her body shook one time after another. Now her hips pounded upward at him and his hand found her tiny clit and he strummed it a dozen times, prolonging her orgasm.

She quieted at last with a long sigh, then she looked at him through half-closed lids.

"My God, Canyon! I could go on that way forever. So marvelous. Tremendous."

"That's just the start," Canyon said, kissing her lips once more, then working his hand down through her soft blond muff over her heartland and down her satin inner thigh. Her legs twitched and jumped as he stroked her tender flesh and the nerves that had just been activated.

"Higher, Canyon, higher. Touch me up higher. Touch mv crotch, now, Canyon. Right now."

His hand went up to her damp, warm lips. They were swollen and red and already coated with lubrication.

"Touch me, Canyon!"

He let his fingers run over them a moment, and her hips jumped toward him; he caressed her around the very center of her and then gently entered her with a finger.

"Oh, glory," she wailed. "It feels so wonderful." Her legs parted and her knees lifted, opening herself to him—offering, giving, presenting—and he lay beside her waiting, watching.

She caught at his manhood and pulled him. "Now, Canyon. Right now, please. Show me what making love is all about."

He eased across her alabaster sleek leg and poised over her. He wet his lance to make it easier, then edged toward her nether lips. They had swollen more and showed more wetness. He touched the soft lips and edged forward.

She cried out in surprise, then a moment of pain and then joy and ecstasy.

"More, Canyon, more!'

He thrust forward and slipped into her velvet sheath in one stroke that brought a warble of surprise and accomplishment. Their flesh came together and bones ground and they were locked together.

"Wonderful, Canyon. Never leave me, never come out of me." She trilled and hummed a little song and then slowly her hips began to thrust upward. No one had to tell her what to do.

She pushed and went back, stroked against him, and slowly he met her thrusts with his own. The pace quickened and her breath came in gasps and then gushes, and soon she screeched at the top of her voice. Her hips pounded him high in the air and held him there for two, three, then four beats before she sighed and dropped on the bed, her arms around his shoulders.

Wendy couldn't talk. She looked at him and smiled and kissed him and hugged him to her, but no words could get through her surging powerhouse of emotions.

Canyon had surged right along with her and blasted his load during her highest point of orgasm, and now he relaxed with her, resting most of his weight on his knees and elbows.

She writhed below him for one last moment, then gave a long sigh, and he thought she was sleeping.

Slowly she began to hug at him with her internal muscles.

She opened her eyes and smiled at him. "Again," she said.

Canyon laughed softly. "Easy for you to do, but I need about ten minutes to rest."

"What a fine way to rest," she said.

They at last got dressed just before five o'clock.

"We can't go down for dinner unless we put on some clothes, I'd guess," Wendy said.

"True, and they won't bring us a meal in our room."

"What are we doing tomorrow?" Wendy said.

"You mean after we make love?"

Wendy nodded. "Only twice tomorrow. What, then?"

"You promised me once a guided tour of the city. You know it like your hometown."

"Yes, I'll be glad to." She slipped the dress on and he buttoned up the front for her.

"This week is going to go by too quickly," Canyon said.

"And then we'll be off on new assignments."

"Or wait and see what President Lincoln wants us to do."

"But we won't worry about that for the next week."

Canyon watched this bright, beautiful girl with the long blond hair and soft brown eyes. She had saved his life yesterday. She would be a good agent one day.

As they walked down to the dining room, he did wonder what his next assignment would be. Wondered just where he would go and what he would do. He was a United States special agent, and proud of it. He would go wherever the president sent him. Even so, as he held a chair for Wendy, he still wondered just what his next assignment would be.

CANYON O'GRADY RIDES ON